Bound in the Arms of a Thug

Chop and Kendyl's Love Story

K.L. Hall

B. Love Publications

Synopsis

Kendyl

I never understood Cy's world.

He belonged to The Spades motorcycle club. To them, he went by Chop.

He told me once he was the sergeant at arms. I'm not sure what that meant either.

All I knew was I'd fallen hard, but I wouldn't stick around as long as he put his MC before me.

If life has taught me anything, it's to leave before you get left.

After I left town, I learned I was three months pregnant with his child.

Chop's decisions had made it clear he wasn't ready for a family, so I kept it from him.

Four years later, I'm working hard to raise my son, who is the spitting image of his father.

But Chop made his choice, and I made mine.

That is until some unexpected chaos forces me back into his arms.

One look, and I can tell he wasn't expecting to see me at his doorstep again.

Neither was the half-naked woman in his living room.

Chop

I never wanted to see Kendyl again after she left and took my heart with her.

Now, she shows up on my doorstep with my son, asking for my help.

As furious as I am, the bruises on her sweet brown skin have me seeing red.

No one lays a hand on my girl.

I don't want to have feelings for her again. I should hate her for what she did, but I can't.

She's the mother of my seed, and the woman who's always had the key to my heart.

I can't blame her for leaving how she did.

But now that I know about my son, I'm never letting them go again.

Trigger Warning:

This book contains instances and/or mentions of domestic violence, abuse, and explicit language that may be triggering for some readers. If you or someone you know is experiencing domestic violence, please seek help from a trusted friend, family member, or a local support organization. Reader discretion is advised.

Kendyl Parker

Four years earlier.

"Mmm, shit! Right there, baby! D-don't s-stop! I-I'm c-cumming," I purred as my stiletto nails clawed at Cy's back.

The bright morning sun filtered through the sheer curtains, casting golden hues against his rich milk chocolate skin. He pumped harder and faster with his eyes half-closed, lost in the sensation of his climax.

"Oooh shit," he growled before spilling his seed inside me.

Our bed—soft and worn—held our naked, tangled limbs. I lay on my side, lazily tracing circles on his brown skin while slowing my heartbeat to a normal rhythm. Rounds of mind-blowing, back-breaking sex was my *favorite* way to wake up in the morning, hands down. His full lips curved into a natural smile before he rolled onto his stomach. His smile was a rare gift. It started in his soft cocoa-brown eyes, crinkling at the corners and spreading to his lips. It was a sunrise breaking through dark storm clouds—the epitome of Black boy joy. His long, dark locs with brown tips cascaded down his ink-stained back. Each strand, freshly hand-twisted by me, held memories of our conversations, lust-filled sunrises, and rain-soaked rides on the back of his motorcycle. Tiny beads and shells adorned a few of his locs, clicking softly whenever he moved. My fingertips skated over the curve of his broad shoulder, connecting imaginary dots before moving to map out imaginary galaxies on his back.

"Baby?"

"Yeah?" he asked, voice thick as he turned to face me.

His goatee and beard were meticulously groomed, perfectly framing his wide, pink lips and strong jawline. His slim, slightly pointed nose added character to his smooth, handsome face. His chocolate brown eyes sparkled under the sunlight. Cy's body was lean and athletic, like an African God. His firm, tatted shoulders bore my scratches of passion and the weight of experiences—both burdens and triumphs.

"I wish—"

Before I could finish my sentence, his phone buzzed on the nightstand next to a faded photograph of us, arms enveloping each other as we laughed against the backdrop of his motorcycle. He grabbed it, and the screen illuminated with the words "*Harlow-Spades MC.*"

My heart galloped. "Don't answer it, baby. Stay here with me," I begged, my fingers skating gracefully down his arm.

I was bound to him by gravity and desire, yet there always seemed to be something pulling him away from me.

"I have to. It's the club. Something might be wrong."

Cy's voice resonated like a cello—deep, soulful, and rich. Whenever he spoke, his words flowed like a slow melody. Each syllable was always deliberate as if he were savoring the taste of each word. His accent was a fusion between the Chicago streets and his Caribbean ancestral roots. He slipped out of bed, reaching for his boxers as his feet hit the wooden floor. I cast my gaze across the room, orbs freezing on the leather jacket hanging on a hook behind the door, the scent of oil clinging to it.

"They always pull you away at the worst times. Can't we just be... here, now?"

"Kendyl, you know I'd stay if I could. But the club—they're my family. They need me."

"What about me? I need you, too! I'm serious, Cy. I can't take this shit anymore. Every day, you're risking your life, riding with that fuckin' biker gang."

"We ain't a fuckin' gang!" he yelled, cutting me off. "What I tell you about that shit?"

I sighed. "Whatever they are, why can't you just leave them behind? We can leave the city and get as far away from Chicago as possible, just the two of us."

"Baby, it's not that simple. The Spades are my brothers. They've got my back when no one else does."

My brows wrinkled in frustration as I shot him a stern glare. "Growing up how I grew up, I understand loyalty, Cyrus Bailey. I do. But what about us? What about *our* future? I can't keep waiting for you to choose between me and them! You know I have abandonment issues. Every time you walk out that door with that jacket on your back, it tears me apart. Can't you see that?" I challenged, tears filling the corners of my eyes.

He stopped moving about the room when I spoke. He leaned back and crossed his arms. His deep brown eyes never wavered like the roots of an ancient tree. He absorbed every tear and shade of my feelings—the fear, disappointment, and sadness. He was a master at reading between the lines. Cy rarely raised his voice. Even in anger, it remained a low rumble like a storm brewing on the horizon.

"You don't understand," he responded slowly. "It's more than riding bikes and fuckin' the city up. We protect our turfs and our neighborhoods. We're a brotherhood bound by loyalty. If I leave, they won't take it lightly. And they *won't* let me go without consequences."

"Consequences?" I queried, voice raising. "Nigga, I'm your girlfriend! I've stood by you through everything—the bar fights, the late nights, the shootouts. But *this*? This is too fuckin' much. You're choosing them over me again, just like you always do!"

"Can you please listen and try to see things from my fuckin' perspective? I've seen things—real dark fuckin' shit, Kendyl. I can't just walk away. It's not a job I can quit. They're my brothers, and I can't abandon them. It's not about picking them over you; it's about finding the balance between both worlds—the calm and the chaos."

Tears rolled down my cheeks. I looked over my shoulder at our carved initials in the headboard—C & K—marked the center. We etched them during a drunken moonlit night, sealing our fate the night he gave me the spare key to his place. Our bedroom had gone from a sanctuary—a place where love met desire, to a cage.

"Balance? If you were worried about balance, we wouldn't be having this conversation right now. But fuck it. You're right. I thought we had something real. It's clear you're choosing your gang over love." I scoffed. "Maybe I should have known better."

He approached my side of the bed and reached out for me. "Kendyl, please—" His phone rang again. He glanced at the screen as a sigh escaped his soft lips. "Baby, I have to take this. It's urgent."

I scoffed. "Of course it is."

His fingers, long and calloused, tapped rhythmically against the top of the headboard as if he were warring with himself about whether to say something or let it go. Instead, he leaned in to kiss my forehead, a promise etched in the simplest gesture.

"I'll be back, Kendyl. Always."

"Fine. Go. But when you come back, I *won't* be here," I threatened, this time for real.

And then he was gone, phone pressed to his ear as the bedroom door closed behind him. I leaned back against the pillow that had once cradled his head and clung to the warmth his melanin-rich skin left behind. In the quiet of the room, I listened to the distant rumble of Cy's motorcycle. I raced to the window, heart sinking amongst the scented candles—vanilla, sandalwood, and rainwater—on the windowsill. His motorcycle roared down the city street, drowning out my heartbeat.

The moment Cyrus left me to run to The Spades changed our relationship profoundly. My trust in him wavered. Whenever I thought about our future, I wondered if he'd always prioritize the club over me. Every time we were tangled in the sheets, he whispered about "forever" when he was deep inside me, but reality always had a way of intruding. The ache of abandonment and resentment pinged my chest—the burn of being second to the club. I wrapped my arms around myself, wondering if love should hurt this damn much. His silence as he left spoke louder than any vow. He'd chosen his life, and if we were going to stay together, I had to accept it. I looked in the full-length mirror across the room, faced with my own choice: stay or leave.

I paced the tattered rug covering the reclaimed wooden floor, its patterns faded but still clinging to life. I imagined cutting the threads and metaphorically setting myself free. My eyes pinged from the nightstand to the overstuffed closet, where my clothes spilled out, colors bleeding into each other. I trekked over to the dresser—scarred but sturdy. My jewelry box rested on the corner. I unhooked the clasp to the silver locket he'd given me and left it there. As if wings had been placed on my feet, I stormed over to the nightstand and snatched my stack of books—poetry, Black romance, and urban fantasy. All the things I'd read aloud to Cy, my voice a lullaby after one of his long days. I tossed them on the bed before yanking open the closet door and pulling out my suitcase. After emptying my dresser drawer and shoving all my hanging dresses inside my luggage, I barreled down the hall into the tiny bathroom, where my collection of scented candles lined the edge of the porcelain tub. I snatched them all.

The fridge hummed quietly inside our small kitchenette, with barely enough space for two people. Its door was adorned with magnets from places we'd been on the back of his bike. I scoffed, snatching the mismatched set of plates stacked on the cabinet shelf. By the time I was done, I wanted the apartment to look like I'd never lived there. I cast my gaze into the living room, where the worn-out couch dominated the space. Its black leather was cracked and sagged in the middle. A coffee table stood in front of the couch, stacked with motorcycle magazines and a half-empty whiskey bottle. I zoomed by the record player resting on a wooden crate in the corner. Vinyl records leaned against the wall—jazz, blues, and old Bob Marley songs. I paused as the memory of Cy spinning the records and us swaying together, getting lost in the smooth melodies that bridged our differences—his rough with my soft.

Growing up, I never knew what love from a real family was. I'd been a product of the system since I was five when my mother decided she loved crack cocaine more than she loved me. Between adolescence and adulthood, anybody who claimed to love me either hurt me or did me wrong. And the few people I loved always ended up leaving me. When I met Cy, I fell hard and fast. Our souls collided like a hurricane and tornado. He was my first dose of stability in this cruel world. We'd been together for over a year, and I thought I'd found forever with him. I thought I could deal with him being a part of a MC, but his world was too much for me. I believed him when he said he loved me, but at what cost?

Once I made sure the only thing of mine left behind were memories, I stormed out of the apartment, lugging my suitcase behind me. The door slammed shut, and I fled, tires screeching as my heart shattered into a million pieces. I drove for hours until the city lights blurred behind me, and all I could see ahead was a star-studded highway. I wanted as much distance as possible between us. Beyond the city, the hills rose like ancient mountains. Their green slopes softened the harsh edges of all the ink and steel I was used to. A smile stretched across my face as I imagined escaping to a place where I could smell the freedom in the air. I didn't know what the road ahead had in store for me—if Cy and I would eventually find our way back to each other or if the divide between us would continue to widen. *Only time will tell.*

Cyrus "Chop" Bailey

I stepped inside the house at two o'clock—the time of morning when most of the world slept, and the stars seemed to hold their breath. I flipped on the lights and stood in the doorway. The apartment was eerily silent, devoid of the familiar sounds—the soft hum of the refrigerator, the distant traffic outside, and most importantly, her laughter. One look around the apartment, and my heart dropped to my stomach. I didn't yell. I didn't even speak. I pelted down the hallway, checking behind every door—the bathroom, the bedroom. Kendyl was gone, vanished like a wisp of smoke, leaving behind only the silver locket I'd given her on our first anniversary. Its delicate chain lay on the dresser, silent proof of her departure. My fingers traced the cool empty sheets, memories flooding back—her laughter on the back of my motorcycle, our traded secrets under moonlit skies, and the warmth of her body pressed against mine. But now that she was gone, the emptiness in the room mirrored the hollowness in my chest. The silence wrapped around everything —the couch, the bed, the shower—as if the night was listening to my sorrow.

I didn't hesitate. I called her phone, which repeatedly went to voicemail, before calling in reinforcements. The Spades were my family, bound by loyalty and leather. I made the call to Harlow, the president, and then my boy Nitro, our road captain, with urgency in my voice as I informed him of the situation.

"Nitro!" I barked into the phone. "We gotta gather the men and tell 'em to hit the streets. Kendyl's gone. She packed all her shit and left no note. I need every pair of eyes out there searching for her. She can't just disappear on me like this!"

Nitro was a few years older than me. He was a rugged biker with the type of scars that told engaging stories. He'd seen it all—brawls, turf wars, and broken hearts. But this was different. I'd never felt this type of desperation before. Love was a dangerous thing, especially when it walked right out the fuckin' front door.

"Chop," his voice crackled through the phone. "I get it. But listen, you stay your ass where you at. Guard that apartment like a fuckin' hawk. She might come back confused or scared. Women do that emotional ass shit sometimes. You know how the game go."

My grip tightened on the phone. "No. She wouldn't just leave. Not without a word. I've been callin' her and can't reach her. She wouldn't do a nigga like this, Nitro. Not after everything we've been through."

He sighed into the receiver. "Look, bruh, I've seen enough heartache to fill a thousand whiskey bottles. Sometimes love's a wild, crazy ride, and sometimes it's a dead-end, *Nightmare on Elm Street-type* shit. But you gotta trust me on this. You stay your ass at that apartment. If she comes back, you'll be there. If she doesn't, well... we'll find her."

My thoughts ran rapidly in my head. I pictured Kendyl's wild, curly hair, the way she smiled wide and laughed when we rode together, her delicate arms wrapped around me. I couldn't lose her— not like this.

I grunted. "Nah. I can't just sit here, nigga. What if she's hurt? What if—"

"Chop, listen. We're brothers, right? We've ridden through the flames of hell and back. But sometimes, this love shit takes a different kind of fight. You fight that shit with patience, nigga, not fists. You stay put. We'll comb every street, every bar, every damn alley if we have to. But you wait. All right?"

I hesitated, then nodded, acknowledging he was right even though I was the only one in the room. "Fine. But if you find her, you call me. No matter what."

His wise voice softened through the receiver. "Bet. Hold your head, nigga. I'll be in touch."

As the line went dead, I paced the floor, my phone clutched tightly, as I left one desperate voicemail after another on her phone that echoed into the void.

Three hours dragged by—an eternity of uncertainty. I stayed put, staring at the empty doorway of our apartment, praying she'd walk back through it at any moment. The silence cocooned the soft shuffle of my insomniac footsteps. Beneath it lay the rapid pulsing of my heartbeat. I continued to replay our last argument, dissecting every word, every teary-eyed glance. Kendyl had threatened to leave me a thousand times. I never thought she'd fuck around and do that shit. The lyrics to Jay-Z's "Song Cry" played back in my head: *I know the way a nigga livin' was wack. But you don't get a nigga back like that.* Had I finally pushed her away? She'd grown tired of my rugged edges and the danger that clung to me like a second skin. I swiped the half-empty bottle of whiskey off the coffee table and chugged it as if it were a bottle of ice-cold water. The liquor had my mind scattered, conjuring up scenarios—accidents, kidnappings, betrayal. When exhaustion finally claimed me, I collapsed on the couch, her locket necklace still clenched in my fist.

I woke up to the harsh light of the afternoon, disoriented as fuck, and my locs disheveled. After taking a shower, my first stop was her job. The news was a cruel blow—she'd quit over the phone, leaving no trace behind, not even a forwarding address for her final check.

"Fuck!" I growled as defeat settled over me like a dark cloud.

I headed back to my motorcycle when my phone rang. Nitro's gruff voice was on the other end. Our men had found her holed up in a plain motel six and a half hours away. Relief surged through me, but I knew better than to rush in. Kendyl was and had always been a wild creature, skittish and wounded by her past. Instead, I instructed them to watch, wait, and give her space. I needed answers. I *craved* them. *Why the fuck did she leave my side? What really drove her away?* The silver locket necklace rested around my neck as I drove toward her, the miles stretching like an endless black ribbon of dull asphalt. When the time was right, I'd return it to her. All I needed to do was lay my eyes on her. Then I'd worry about confronting her and maybe figure out how to piece together the shattered fragments of our relationship.

As my motorcycle roared into the small town, I felt the weight of the locket against my chest—a silent reminder of our connection that I hoped wasn't too broken. The motel appeared ahead, its neon vacancy sign flickering in the night. I parked in the shadows, the engine's growl fading to a low hum. My approach had to be delicate, like handling a fragile kitten. Kendyl was as unpredictable as the weather. I couldn't storm in, guns blazing. No, this required finesse and patience. I leaned against my bike, scanning the motel's entrance. The curtains twitched in one of the windows, revealing her beautiful silhouette. I saw her eyes—guarded and haunted. My heart's cadence bordered on wild. She was there, close yet impossibly distant. I wondered which of my demons had chased her this far and what secrets she held behind that door.

My boys were positioned discreetly, watching and waiting. They knew the rules: no sudden moves, no confrontations—just surveillance. I'd play the long game and keep my distance, waiting for the right moment to step in and reclaim what was rightfully mine.

Kendyl

Six months slipped by since I vanished from Cy's life, leaving behind an apartment and a throbbing heartache that refused to dull. Once exciting and sweet, memories of our love still clung to me like ivy on an old brick wall. Sometimes, in the middle of the night, I could still feel the warmth of his hand in mine or hear his laughter from behind the shower curtain when the water ran. But I made a choice—a painful yet necessary choice for my future—to leave before I was left. But every time I walked into my doctor's appointments alone, I wondered if it was the right one. Did he regret the words left unsaid as much as I did? Or had he already moved on and found someone new to warm his bed?

As the seasons changed, so did my body. The secret I carried within me grew, hidden beneath layers of silence and solitude. I definitely hadn't planned it this way—unknowingly almost three months pregnant when I left, my heart torn between love and fear—love for the life growing inside me and fear of a future with Cy that I couldn't predict. The fear of being rejected ate away at me. I traced the curve of my belly, feeling the flutter of life beneath my fingertips, and wondered how things would be if I'd stayed and he'd known. Thoughts of him weighed heavier on my mind than usual because it was his birthday. I reached for my phone, hesitating, before I unlocked it. I still had his number blocked on my old phone, and I had completely changed my number. *Should I send a message? A simple "Happy birthday" to bridge the gap between all the lost time? No. It's better this way. Safer. For him, for me, for our unborn child.* I closed my eyes, imagining him out there in the world. Was he out somewhere in a drunken stupor celebrating with his boys? Or was he alone, like me, sitting on the cushioned chair inside the waiting room of my obstetrician's office?

My hands rested on my swollen belly, feeling the strong kicks of my unborn son. The space was painted in soothing pastels, and the soft hum of the air conditioner provided some relief from the spring heat. I glanced at the clock on the wall—my weekly appointment was eleven minutes overdue. The other expectant mothers chatted quietly, their eyes occasionally darting toward the door. Suddenly, I felt a tightness in my lower abdomen. It wasn't the usual Braxton Hicks contractions or the familiar ache of period cramps I was used to; this was different. I shifted in my seat, trying to ease the discomfort. My heart raced. *Is this it?* The cramps gripped my stomach, radiating through my pelvis and back. The ache was relentless, building in intensity as the minutes passed.

Just then, the nurse appeared in the doorway, clipboard in her hand. Her smile faded when she saw my pained expression. "Ms. Parker, are you okay?"

I gripped the armrests. "Something's not right. It's like a constant cramp, and it's getting stronger," I replied, sucking in air through my teeth.

The nurse's eyes widened. "Let me get Doctor Rodriguez." She hurried down the hallway, leaving me alone with my rapid thoughts. Panic surged through me. *Is it too early?* I hadn't even gotten around to packing my hospital bag. Moments later, my OB swept into the waiting room, her white coat flapping behind her like a superhero cape. Her calm demeanor provided the reassurance I didn't even know I needed. "Kendyl, what's going on? Talk to me."

My voice trembled. "I'm having these pains, Doctor. They're getting more and more intense."

Dr. Rodriguez guided me to my feet. "Let's check. Let's get you into an exam room." I waddled down the hallway and settled on the paper-covered surface on the examination table. Dr. Rodriguez checked my cervix. "Kendyl, you're already five centimeters dilated. You're in active labor," she stated, confirming my worst nightmare.

My eyes ballooned as panic seized me. "But it's too early! My due date is still three weeks away!"

Dr. Rodriguez's expression softened. "Sometimes, our little ones have their own schedules, and your little bundle of joy is eager to meet his mommy." She glanced at the nurse who was standing by the door. "Call Labor and Delivery. We need to get Kendyl to the hospital."

"On it," she replied before exiting the room.

All the frantic thoughts in my mind jumbled up, causing my brain to fog. Going into labor was the *last* thing I expected, especially on Cy's birthday. *Of course, I'd go into labor on his birthday.* Fate always had a way of linking us together every time I tried to sever the ties. I hadn't even packed my hospital bag or finished assembling the crib, all the things I knew he would've handled had he been around or known at all.

"Is my son going to be okay?" I asked, panic laced in my voice.

Dr. Rodriguez patted my hand. "We'll take good care of you both. You're in capable hands."

The nurse reappeared with a wheelchair and wheeled me out of the office. I clung to my belly as if shielding my unborn child from the world's uncertainties. The waiting room blurred as I passed by the expecting mothers, one in particular who mouthed, *"Good luck."* I nodded, my pulse racing as I managed a weak smile through the pain. The nurse wheeled me into the elevator and across the sterile corridor into the hospital. The labor pains intensified, each contraction a reminder of my solitude.

I contemplated calling Cy, telling him the truth, begging him to come and coach me through the pain. I'd hold the baby in and keep him from coming out until he got to me if I had to. When I used to think about our future, I imagined giving birth with him by my side, whispering words of encouragement, and sharing the joy of meeting our son for the first time. I closed my eyes, forcing the tears to stay at bay. *I can't call him into the middle of my chaos now. I won't.* But the ache of loneliness was relentless. It gnawed at my insides, a hunger that couldn't be satisfied or drowned out. I missed him all the time, but especially during my labor. Our love was a natural disaster, beautiful and destructive. We were fire and ice, passion and pain, sugar and steel. Ultimately, I chose to douse the flames and walk away from the inferno I knew would consume us both.

THE WALLS IN THE DELIVERY ROOM WERE BARE, NO ARTWORK— just sterile white surfaces, a blank canvas for my birth story. Standing tall beside the bed was an IV pole. The thin tubes snaked their way to my arm, carrying fluids. The sensors from the fetal monitor rested on my belly, tracking the baby's heartbeat and each contraction. Against the opposite wall sat an empty chair. It was where Cy was expected to sit while holding my hand and witnessing the miracle of childbirth unfold in front of him. His presence was supposed to be my lifeline, but I had to be my own anchor.

My contractions came in waves, each spiking higher than the last. They demanded my attention, leaving no room for distraction or sporadic thoughts of Cy. Walking, talking, and rational thought became luxuries I couldn't afford. The pain switched between stabbing like lightning and aching like an old wound. By the time they'd gotten me checked in and hooked up to all the monitors, I was too far dilated for an epidural. I had no choice but to draw strength from my primal instincts and surrender to the pained dance of labor. The doctor and nurses flooded the room, ready to guide me through the sacred threshold of motherhood, one breath at a time. I swayed between agony and anticipation, pushing through the agony as tears streamed down my face.

After five hard pushes, the baby emerged—a tiny, fragile, screaming being, brown eyes squinting against the harsh light. And there, in that moment of raw vulnerability, I caught a glimpse of his melanated features—the same eyes, the exact curve of the lips. He looked like his father, the man I'd loved and left. I cradled my newborn son against my chest, thirsty for skin-to-skin contact. Suddenly, the pain was worth every second. As happy as I was to meet him finally, my heart ached for a different reason. Tears slid down my cheeks as I wept for the life the three of us could have had—the family dinners, bedtime stories, and shared memories. I wept for the love that had slipped through my fingers like sand, leaving only memories and unanswered questions. The baby stirred, his tiny brown fingers curling around mine. I kissed his forehead, imprinting my unconditional love on his soft skin. Together, we faced an uncertain future where I would be navigating the tides of single motherhood with no roadmap.

"Happy birthday, Cree Anthony Parker. I'm your mommy. It's you and me against the world." And as he nestled against my warm chest, I vowed to be both mother and father, protector and guide.

Kendyl

P*resent day.*

IT WAS WELL PAST TEN O'CLOCK AT NIGHT. I SAT COMFORTABLY on my well-loved, slightly worn-out sofa, wearing mismatched PJs. The cushions bore the imprint of countless bedtime stories and late-night Cree and Mommy cuddle sessions. My legs were outstretched and crossed, pedicured toes resting on the sturdy wooden coffee table with a half-finished Spiderman puzzle to one side. I looked down the hallway where the dim nightlight from Cree's half-open bedroom door cast a long shadow across the carpet. *Good. He's still sleeping.*

As I was about to settle into a psychological thriller movie on Netflix, I heard keys jingling in the lock. The hairs on my nape stood at attention. My eyes darted over to Cree's wicker toy chest in the corner. There was a jumble of action figures, building blocks, and miniature cars and trucks scattered around it. *Fuck. Another thing for him to complain about.*

I heard the familiar thud of his boots against the floor. He was here—uninvited, unwelcome. I shot up from the couch, desperate to look busy. The door opened, and I turned to see my boyfriend, Cash Majors—the man who'd once whispered tender promises of love and affection—standing in the doorway, his brooding brown eyes bloodshot and wild. His anger was a tornado, and I always seemed to be the fragile twig caught in its path. I'd hoped and prayed he wouldn't drop by tonight, but of course, fate had other plans.

Cash was a striking figure—a handsome mahogany canvas with debonair features. His jawline was chiseled and unyielding, framing a mouth that spat both honeyed lies and bitter truths. His orbs were like obsidian pools—deep and unreadable. His six-foot frame sauntered inside, and it was as if the earth itself bent to his will.

"Kenny!" His voice was a venomous hiss, slicing through the movie dialogue. "Where the fuck is my dinner? You think a nigga works his ass off all day to come home to an empty plate?"

My trembling hands clutched the remote, pausing the movie. I'd never regretted giving him my spare key more than I did at the moment. I eased into the kitchen, pausing at the edge of the counter. I'd lost count of how many times I'd cooked for his ass, only to have my efforts dismissed or criticized. I had nothing to offer—no hot meal, no excuses—just exhaustion and fear.

"Cash, please," I whispered, my voice barely audible. "Please don't wake up Cree. And I'm sorry about the food. I—I didn't expect you."

He staggered toward me, the stench of alcohol clinging to his leather jacket. His chocolate brown eyes bore into mine, pupils dilated with rage. "*Sorry?*" His laugh was bitter. "You're always fuckin' sorry, Kendyl. But sorry doesn't put food on the table, does it? And a nigga still hungry."

His hand shot out, striking my cheek with a force that sent me reeling. The pain bloomed, sharp and searing like a fresh bee sting. I instantly tasted coppery blood. My lip had split from the impact. I stumbled backward, my back hitting the kitchen wall. My gaze darted to my cell phone on the counter—the lifeline I had yet to use.

"You think you can leave me, bitch?" Cash's voice dropped to a dangerous whisper. "After all I've done for you?"

My mind raced. I'd tried to break free before, but his grip tightened each time. My coworkers at the private doctor's office where I worked saw me as a strong, independent Black woman who always smiled and never complained. They didn't know about the bruises hidden beneath my long sleeves or the nights I spent crying and screaming into my pillow, fed up with the way my life was going.

"Please," I begged, my voice raw. "Cree's sleeping. Just go."

But, of course, he wasn't finished. He leaned in, his liquored breath hot against my face. "You're mine!" he spat. "You'll *always* be mine."

My thoughts screamed at me. *Enough! You can't keep living like this!* But the fear of another blow paralyzed me. I had no family, and the only close friend I had to turn to was my neighbor, Remy, but she wasn't home. Thoughts of Cree—sweet and innocent—flashed to the front of my mind. He deserved so much better. I couldn't let him witness the darkness inside Cash.

Since leaving Chicago behind, my life had been a delicate balancing act between my day job as a medical billing assistant and my moonlighting gig as a weekend waitress at a hole-in-the-wall bar on 7th Street. About eight months ago, Cash had walked into that bar —a dust storm wrapped in leather and ink from head to toe. His eyes, dark as midnight, had locked onto mine when he appeared out of nowhere to silence the drunk heckler giving me a hard time with a single glance. I watched, heart pounding, as he stood tall, a guardian angel in a sea of chaos. I'd never seen anyone move with such grace and menace, the kind that whispered secrets of danger *and* a hell of a good time. He approached me afterward and asked if I was okay, his voice a low rumble. I nodded, unable to pry my gaze away from his handsome features. One look at him and how he commanded the room, and he was instantly living rent-free in my mind. We exchanged numbers, and the rest was a blur of late-night texts and stolen kisses in the back of the bar.

Initially, he was sweet—a menace with a hard exterior but soft as a teddy bear on the inside. He pulled out all the stops: flowers, candlelit dinners, promises of forever, and a real family for my son. My wounded heart found solace in the warmth of his touch and how he made me feel like the center of the universe. I thought I'd finally found true love again since leaving Cy. But then the mask slipped an inch at a time like a snake shedding its skin. His laughter turned cold, and his gaze lost its tenderness. He became possessive and demanding. The nickname "Demon" echoed through the bar, whispered by patrons who had glimpsed the darkness hiding beneath his charm. They said it started with a bar fight, an eruption of violence that left broken glass and mugshots in its wake. Cash had been the cause of it all, his brooding gaze blazing with fire. In the aftermath—he stared down the room, daring anyone to challenge him. And so, the name "Demon" stuck—a label that clung to him like a curse. Yet, he basked in it and wore it like a coat of armor most days. When I met him, I knew none of this—that he'd be the man who would become both my salvation and my downfall. But as the bruises bloomed on my melanated skin and his facade continued to crack, I knew his nickname held more truth than legend.

My discovery of Cash's dark side unfolded like a slow burn. It started with random mood swings that would cause him to snap at me for no reason. Then I noticed the faint marks on his knuckles—the kind that came from hitting something hard like concrete, glass, or pounding flesh. When I asked, he brushed it off as a bar fight with a rival motorcycle club. When I asked what he meant, he told me not only did he belong to a motorcycle club, but he was also the president. Just when I thought I'd escaped the life of bikers and brawls, I'd been sucked right back into one. But I'd already fallen for him. I was in over my head before I knew it. Perhaps the most memorable discovery was when I burnt dinner. I'd gotten caught up trying to get Cree in the bath when I smelled the scent of burnt meat in the air. Of course, Cash was angry. His rage was visibly etched into his frown and downturned brow. When I tried to reason with him and offer to order a pizza, he struck me—a loud sharp slap that echoed through the apartment. My cheek stung, and I tasted blood. At that moment, I *knew* I was dancing with a demon.

I'd tried to break up with him—told him it was over a month ago when the bruises were still faint crescents on my arms. But he wouldn't allow it. If anything, his grip on me and my life tightened. He whispered threats, promising that I'd never escape him. Because he was the president of the Raging Vipers MC, he had eyes and ears everywhere. And so, I did the only thing I could do—hide the evidence from *everyone* around me. I couldn't let my coworkers, Remy, or my son see the truth.

I traced the contours of my split lip as Cash cornered me between the stove and the fridge. His face was twisted in rage as his six-foot frame towered over me. "Remember that two months of fuckin' back rent I paid?"

"I haven't forgotten, b-baby," I replied, limbs trembling in fear.

I had to take off from both jobs when Cree got sick with strep and back-to-back ear infections. No work meant no pay. My bills started piling up like a stack of cards, and I had no choice but to go to Cash for help, a desperate plea so that I'd keep a roof over our heads.

"You owe me, which means I *own* you," he spat, his voice low and menacing.

His words were like slivers of glass, slicing through my fragile heart. I prayed Cree was still sleeping soundly, blissfully unaware of the storm brewing around him. I'd done everything I could to protect him, but now I was trapped in a nightmare of my creation. I was the one who'd let the devil in.

"Okay. Okay. I'm sorry," I whispered, my voice barely audible.

"You better be. Because if your ass don't learn how to be a good fuckin' woman, I'ma start taking my anger out on your son like my mother's boyfriends did me. Turn that lil nigga into a real man."

Cash's threats echoed in my ears, shifting something within me.

How dare this bitch ass mothafucka threaten my son! The weight of my desperation pressed down on my chest. I sank to my knees, tears of anger and regret streaming down my face.

"I-I'll be better. I p-promise, just don't touch him. *Ever.* Please, just give me another ch-chance," I begged before doing the only thing I knew that would lull his rage. I slowly started to unbuckle his belt and unzip his dusty black jeans. "Let me make it up to you."

A COUPLE OF HOURS LATER, HE LEFT TO DO ANOTHER ONE OF HIS illegal jobs. As the motorcycle club president, his title held power and danger. As the door slammed shut behind him, I lay on the bed, staring at the crackled ceiling. My insomniac mind raced, and something deep within me stirred—the burning instinct to survive, tipping me to my breaking point. And then it came—my inner voice, soft yet insistent. *Run.* The night's shadows whispered an uprising, urging me to break free while I could. If Cash wouldn't leave us the hell alone, then we'd leave him and *never* come back.

I didn't hesitate. I shot out from underneath the covers and threw on a pair of black sweatpants, socks, and a hoodie. I raced around the apartment, gathering what was most precious—enough clothes for at least a couple of weeks, Cree's favorite stuffed animal and action figures, and a faded photograph of happier times of Cree and me on his first birthday at the beach. I threw them all into the car before strapping Cree's sleeping body into his car seat. My heart danced as the engine roared to life. I glanced into my rearview mirror, praying Demon's riders weren't lurking in the shadows. In the quiet of that moment, I vowed never to look back. I drove, powered by panic and grit.

ABOUT TWO HOURS INTO MY DRIVE, MY PHONE BUZZED NONSTOP in the center console. I'd blocked Cash's number early on, knowing he was the last person I'd want to hear from. I glanced at the screen, each vibration feeling like a jolt to my unraveled nerves. I saw Remy's name, and my shoulders relaxed. She was my neighbor. I leaned on her when I was in a pinch and needed someone to watch Cree when I worked late or pulled doubles at the bar. She was probably the one person I trusted—who knew that violence was Cash's love language.

I swiped the screen, answering her call. "Remy," I said, my voice shaky.

"Where are you?" she asked. Her voice was urgent and laced with concern. "I just pulled up and didn't see your car outside."

I hesitated while glancing at the endless stretch of road ahead. "I had to leave," I finally admitted. "Cash—he hit me again, and this time he threatened my son. I couldn't stay there."

Silence hung between us. So much so that I could almost hear Remy's mind racing through the phone, trying to digest the information I'd just dropped on her. "Where are you now?" she asked softly.

"I'm still driving," I answered. "No destination in mind. Just trying to put as much distance between us as possible."

"But you and Cree are safe?" Remy pressed.

"Yes," I said. "For now." I sighed. I didn't mean to let the dread slip past my lips, but it was out in the universe.

"Keep driving," Remy said firmly. "I'll stay on the line with you. We'll talk about whatever you wanna talk about, anything—every-thing—*except* your situation. Anything to keep you awake."

"Okay. Thank you," I replied.

I kept my eyes wide and fixated on the open road, allowing my mind to wander to safer places. As the miles stretched, we talked about happier times—Cree's silly moments, work drama at the bar, and my aspirations to move up at my full-time job. Remy's familiar voice soothed me. She was the sole thread connecting me to sanity and hope.

FOUR AND A HALF HOURS LATER, THE CITY LIGHTS OF CHICAGO welcomed me back. It had been years since I'd returned, but my muscle memory took over as I easily made my way around the city. Soon enough, I parked in front of Cy's apartment, my heart thumping as the morning sun rose. I left the car running as Cree slept, looking over my shoulder every few seconds as I stood on the stoop. My knuckles trembled against the door. When it swung open, revealing an elderly Hispanic woman with kind eyes, I felt relief and curiosity. The woman's silver hair framed her face, and her tired but warm eyes held a lifetime of stories.

"¿En qué puedo ayudarte?" the woman asked, her voice warm yet cautious since it was so early in the morning.

I paused with confusion etched in my brow, unsure how to respond. Truthfully, I had no clue what she said. We stared each other down before I broke away to look back at my car.

"You look like you've been through a storm," she said, returning my attention to her.

I hesitated, remembering my busted lip, then blurted out my question. "I apologize for showing up here so late... er, uh, early. Do you... did you know the man who–who lived here before you?"

The woman's eyes crinkled at the corners. "Ah, sí. A good man. He doesn't live here anymore, but he still visits once a month, like clockwork. Helps fix things around the place."

I squinted, unsure if we were talking about the same man. I'd never known Cy to be the Mr. Fix-It type. "Are you sure? He's about six-foot-two and has dark eyes and dreads."

She leaned in, lowering her voice. "Ah, sí, sí. He's got a motorcycle."

My heart skipped a beat. "Yes! Sí, sí. That's him! Would you know where I could find him? Does he still live around here?"

She wagged her head. "Are you family?"

I glanced back at the car, catching a glimpse of Cree before turning back to face her. "Something like that."

She looked me up and down before peering at my car. "I think he's across the city in the new Oak Creek subdivision."

"Thank you, ma'am. Thank you so much. Again, I'm so sorry to wake you up so early! Gracias!"

"De nada. I hope you find what you're looking for."

The name of the subdivision echoed in my thoughts—a breadcrumb leading me to him. Back inside the car, I did a quick Google search for the subdivision and got an address for the model home in the area. After another twenty-minute drive, I crept through the neighborhood, the streets lined with new, modest townhouses and blooming lawns. And then I saw it—the unmistakable silhouette of a motorcycle—*his motorcycle*—parked in front of a brand-new house.

"Found you," I whispered.

I cut the engine, my palms sweaty on the steering wheel. I glanced in the rearview mirror. Cree still slept in the back seat, blissfully unaware of the drama about to unfold. I stepped out and walked to the back passenger seat to grab him. I cradled him in my arms as my footsteps echoed on the pavement. The dewy morning air smelled of fresh grass as I approached the house. My heart pounded. The green front door loomed before me—a threshold to my past and perhaps my future. As I raised my hand to knock, I wondered what awaited me on the other side. *What if he doesn't recognize me? I wonder how much he's changed. Have time and circumstance transformed him into someone unrecognizable?* I'd been rehearsing what I'd say to him for most of the six-and-a-half-hour drive, but all my words escaped me in the heat of the moment.

I took a deep breath, my knuckles brushing against the wood as I knocked. The door opened, and there he stood—the man who had once loved me and had never raised his hand in anger. Our eyes met, and in that charged moment, the past collided with the present. It'd been four years since I'd laid eyes on Cy, and now it was time to confront the truth—the tangled threads of love, betrayal, and the sleeping toddler in my arms that bound us together.

Chop

The sun had barely stretched its golden fingers across the horizon when the doorbell shattered the slurping sounds of my early morning head session. Grumbling, I tossed the broad off me that I'd met at the clubhouse a few hours prior. I stumbled toward the entrance while pulling up my pants. My head pounded from the previous night's raucous celebration. My MC brothers had toasted my newfound status as a homeowner, and the housewarming party had blurred into a haze of weed, whiskey shots, lap dances, and laughter.

I yanked the door open, shirtless and bleary-eyed, ready to unleash my annoyance on whoever dared disturb me. I was horny as fuck, and I needed the release. But the words died on my lips when I saw Kendyl standing there, her beautiful face a mosaic of pain and desperation. Her once-vibrant chestnut brown eyes were dull, and her swollen, busted lip tarnished her delicate features. I was unexpectedly struck with silence as I shuffled back a step or two.

The sight of her sent a jolt through my chest, a chaotic mix of anger, longing, and worry.

I continued my visual inspection of her body from head to toe. A

"

mountain of questions burned my tongue, especially about the sleeping kid she clutched in her arms—a tiny boy nestled against her chest, oblivious to the turmoil around him. My heart stuttered.

"Kendyl," I spat out her name, the two syllables sharp as shards of glass. "What the *fuck* happened to you?"

Her gaze flickered past mine. I followed her eyes toward the woman who stood a few feet away in the middle of the stairs, her eyes wide with shock. Her messy hair, one-shoulder mini dress, and smudged lipstick told the story of our wild night. As much as I had previously been enjoying my time with her, I no longer had the desire for her company. I looked at the curvy stranger and then back at Kendyl—the woman who'd once held the key to my heart—who was equally unfamiliar. We'd burned bright and crashed hard. Our love was a wildfire that consumed everything in its path, including us.

She flinched, her gaze dropping to the floor. "Cy," she whispered, her voice barely audible. "I... I didn't know where else to go."

My fists clenched at my sides. I wanted to scream, to unleash the fury that had simmered within me for years. But when I looked at her, *really* looked, I saw the exhaustion etched into her features—the shadows under her eyes, the way she swayed slightly on her feet.

I softened my tone. "Kendyl, tell me who did this to you."

She hesitated, then lifted her gaze to meet mine. "Someone dangerous," she answered. "Someone who won't stop until he finds me... finds us."

"Give me a name." Her lips quivered as I stepped closer, my anger momentarily forgotten. "Tell me," I urged. "Tell me, Kendyl."

She shook her head. "Not now," she said. "I need your help. Just for tonight. Please."

My heart warred with my mind. I hadn't seen or heard from Kendyl in years, not since she packed her shit and voluntarily removed herself from my life. She'd disappeared without a trace, leaving me with a gaping hole in my chest. The memories flooded the front of my mind—our laughter, our fights, the way she'd left me without a word. Yet here she was, battered and desperate. How the fuck could I turn away the woman whose silver locket I still wore around my neck?

"Whose kid is this?" I probed, torn between anger and curiosity.

Kendyl's voice trembled. "He's yours, Cy. He's our son."

My entire world tilted on its axis. My mind raced to connect the dots. The child's features—the same head of unruly dark curls I had growing up, the curve of his jaw—mirrored mine. I glanced at the woman behind me, who wore a mix of shock and hurt on her face. I didn't give a fuck about her feelings. As far as I was concerned, she was a casualty of our tangled lives. I had bigger shit to process. My ex had just returned, carrying *my* seed in her arms. As the morning light filtered through the doorway, I faced a reckoning I never saw coming —a chance at fatherhood and a second chance with Kendyl's heart.

My gaze shifted from Kendyl to the woman standing in the middle of my stairwell.

Her presence was suddenly an unwelcome intrusion, starkly contrasting the fragile bundle in Kendyl's arms.

"Yo, you gotta get the fuck out," I told her. My voice was a low growl, my protective instincts flaring.

She took a step back, her mascara-smudged eyes darting between us. "Yeah. I'll leave," she mumbled. "I didn't sign up for this shit."

Her heels clicked against my hardwood floor, echoing against the bare walls. Kendyl shifted to the side, her grip on the child tightening as she allowed the broad to pass. The door slammed behind her, and the child stirred, eyelashes fluttering against his plump cheeks. My heart clenched. I'd never imagined fatherhood like this—unexpected, messy as fuck, and swarming with unfinished business. I glanced at the kid—*our* kid—sleeping peacefully. The boy's tiny brown fingers curled against Kendyl's chest, and my hard exterior shattered like glass. I'd never been good at resisting her, even when common sense screamed otherwise.

"Take 'em upstairs. You two can have my bed. It's upstairs, the last door on the left."

"Thanks."

Kendyl's words echoed up the carpeted stairs, unraveling the threads of my carefully constructed life. I'd just bought a new townhouse and ain't have shit in it but a couch, box spring, and a mattress in this bitch. Now, suddenly, I had to start putting money away into a college fund for the son I never knew I had. *Ain't this about a bitch.*

Kendyl

The carpeted stairs creaked under my 115-pound weight as I descended, the soft glow of the morning light peeking out from underneath the sheet strung up over his front windows guided my way. The house—*his* house, smelled of fresh paint and possibility. The air held a hint of newness, like the fresh pages of an unopened book waiting to be read. The living room lay before me, a blank canvas. No curtains. No blinds. The flat-screen TV hung on the wall, its black surface reflecting the dim light. Beside it was a sleek video game console perched on a makeshift stand. The room felt huge, echoing with emptiness. The only other piece of furniture was a new black leather couch where he sat, its cushions still plump and firm. He finally lived in a decent zip code and was still living ghetto fabulous. I admired his glow-up, though.

I paused on the bottom step and glanced around, taking in the scene—the unpacked boxes and totes stacked in a corner, waiting to reveal their contents. It was a house of beginnings, a space where memories would be etched into the walls for years to come. Cyrus Bailey owned property, which was more than I could say for myself. Compared to him, my ass was straight-up losing. The only thing I had going for me was our beautiful son. Cree was the best thing that had ever happened to me.

Staring down his father again after so many years made me feel selfish for keeping the gift of Cree all to myself for so long. My cheeks burned with shame. I thought I was doing the right thing, but looking around, I felt a lump of regret in my throat that I couldn't swallow. I cleared my throat, which made him turn to me.

"Did you just move in?" I quizzed, obviously avoiding the elephant in the room.

"Yeah, about a week ago. You never did tell me how you found out where I lived. Only my club members know where I live."

"I went back to our... your old place. The old woman there told me the name of your subdivision, and Google did the rest," I replied.

His brows dipped low. "Mrs. Rodriguez?"

"I didn't get her name, but yeah, sure. She spoke highly of you," I mentioned.

"She's cool. I sublet the apartment to her a few months back and just couch-surfed until this finished getting built."

"Congratulations, by the way," I said softly, my voice cracking. "What made you wanna become a homeowner?"

"Nigga gotta grow up someday, right?"

I shrugged before tearing my gaze down to the floor, allowing my hair to hide my face. "Yeah. I guess you're right about that."

His eyes met mine, and I saw the mix of pride and uncertainty in his gaze. I knew he'd worked hard for it—a place to call his own, a sanctuary. But it lacked warmth, the touch of a woman's hand to soften its edges. I assumed he preferred it that way. He stepped away, leaving me standing halfway between the couch and the front door.

He returned a few minutes later, clutching a bag of frozen peas. "Here. Put that shit on your lip."

I briefly closed my eyes. I knew I had to look hideous. I pressed the cold peas against my swollen lip, wincing. "Thanks."

"Yeah."

I cleared my throat to slice through the deafening silence

between us. All I heard was the *Jeopardy* theme music playing in the back of my mind as we both waited for the other to make the next move.

Finally, Cy sighed. "So, we gon' talk about the elephant in the room now or later?"

My chest deflated with a hard breath I didn't even know I'd been holding. "I know you want answers."

"Fuck want. I *deserve* answers, Kendyl. Why the fuck didn't you tell me I had a son? And then, after everything, you show up like this? Tell me what the fuck is going on!"

"I left him," I began, my voice trembling. "My ex. He was dangerous and unpredictable. He threatened to hurt our son, and I couldn't bear the thought of my baby suffering because of my poor choices."

His eyes narrowed, anger simmering just beneath the surface. "Why didn't you come to me before now? Why keep our son a secret?"

I hesitated, my pride warring with vulnerability as I dropped my chin to my chest. "I was scared," I confessed. "Scared that you'd choose your motorcycle club over us like you always used to do. Scared that our son would be caught in the crossfire."

His jaw clenched, and I saw the pain etched into the lines of his handsome face. "You don't know how wrong you were," he said, his voice low and gravelly. "I would have given up everything for you both."

I wanted to believe him, to let his words wash away the guilt that consumed me. But the past couldn't be rewritten, and my choices had consequences. I'd hidden our son, believing it was the best path —a frantic choice fueled by fear of abandonment and heightened emotions. He stepped closer, his gaze piercing through my defenses.

"You think you made the right choice?" he asked, his voice like a blade. "Leaving me in the dark, denying me the chance to be a father to my kid?"

I swallowed hard, my throat dry. "I thought it was the only way," I whispered hoarsely. "I thought I was protecting him."

Cy's hand slowly reached out, cupping my chin, and I winced as his thumb grazed my swollen lip. "You don't get to decide what's best for us alone," he said, his touch both gentle and punishing. "*Our* son deserved better."

I wanted to apologize, to beg for forgiveness, but my pride held my tongue hostage. Instead, I changed the subject, seeking asylum in unexciting details. "Can I take a shower?" I questioned, my voice small like a child.

He nodded, his expression unreadable. We stood in a silent stand-off for about thirty seconds before he spoke up. "There are two bathrooms upstairs. The one in the hall and the other in my room. I'll get you a fresh towel."

"Thanks."

I decided to use the hall bathroom to ensure I didn't wake Cree's last few moments of peace in Cy's room. I gently closed the door behind me and rested my palm against it before slowly turning around. I walked over to reach behind the curtain and turned on the shower to allow the water to heat up. The water in the shower drummed against the tiles, a rhythmic beat that matched the turmoil in my chest as I stripped bare.

The bathroom mirror reflected a fractured version of myself, holding no mercy. My tired eyes, once bright and hopeful, were now hollow. Dark circles clung to the delicate skin beneath them, evidence of the sleepless hours I'd spent driving and agonizing over my choices. My cheeks were drained of life, and my matted curls drooped around my face. But it was the lip, that assaulted curve of flesh, that drew my attention. My swollen, ugly, busted lip stood out like a crimson badge of shame. The bruised skin, mottled with shades of purple and red, traced the contours of my mouth. It was a cruel reminder of the violence I'd endured from Cash.

I pressed my fingertips gently against the tender flesh, wincing as pain shot through me. The split in my lip seemed to echo the rift that had torn my life apart. Tears flooded my sunken cheeks. My shoulders shook as I sobbed, allowing my pain to pour out after keeping it bottled in for so long. I pressed my hand to my mouth, muffling the sobs that threatened to escape. I prayed the bathroom walls absorbed my agony and that no one wouldn't hear my cries beyond the door.

Then, the door cracked open. Cy stood there holding a fresh towel. Our eyes locked, and time folded in on itself. I didn't even bother covering myself or my bruises. Instead of closing the door and leaving me to fall apart in peace, he dropped the towel, stepped inside, and eased the door shut. He stepped closer to me, and my heart swelled with a bizarre mix of emotions. My heart, battered and carefully locked away, now beat wildly against its cage with every passing second I stood in his presence. The memories flooded back—our laughter, the way he'd held me at night as if he never wanted to let me go. But alongside the nostalgia, there was pain. Pain for the years lost, the words left unsaid, and the romantic love that had withered like a forgotten flower.

I held out my hand to stop him. "I-I-I'm o-ok–okay," I sobbed, trying to talk through my tears.

He swatted my hand out of the way and crashed his body into mine. Our first hug after four long years was a rollercoaster of sweet memories and gut-twisting emotions. The steamy air between us seemed to hold its breath as if the universe recognized the moment's impact. I lay against his chest, hearing his heartbeat echoing in my ear. His embrace was solid, familiar, yet foreign. His scent—a blend of musk and something uniquely him—enveloped me.

I buried my face in the curve of his neck, inhaling deeply, still trying to fight the urge to continue falling apart. My tears were hot against his skin. His hands settled on my lower back, strong and gentle. I felt the tension in his muscles, the restraint he imposed on himself. Four years of absence, four years of silence, and now we stood there, clinging to the frayed edges of a love that had never truly died.

I'd imagined that moment countless times—our reunion, Cree's adolescent laughter filling the gaps between us. But reality surpassed anything my imagination could conjure. His heartbeat matched mine, a rhythm that spoke of our shared history and unspoken apologies. He pulled back slightly, his eyes searching mine. The lines around his eyes had deepened, etched by time. Without saying a word, he scooped me into his arms and put me inside the shower.

Cy stepped in behind me, shirtless but with his basketball shorts and one sock covering his foot. I stepped under the spray, letting it cascade over my body. The warmth couldn't wash away the shame or the humiliation. I closed my eyes, allowing the water to blur my vision, the memories, and the pain—everything, really. As Cy gently washed my body, I allowed myself to cry. Silent tears mingled with the warm shower spray, slipping down my cheeks and disappearing down the drain. He continued washing me from head to toe while inspecting the bruises all over my body. He didn't care about the water saturating his locs. He didn't try to take advantage of me by staking his claim on my body. All he did was wash me clean. Amongst the sea of tattoo ink splattered against his skin or the water sliding down his washboard abs, I noticed the silver locket I'd left lying on that dresser lying against his chest.

"Y-you kept it?" I mumbled, eyes clinging to droplets on the locket.

"I haven't taken it off since you left," he admitted.

"Did you look for me?"

"I found you."

"What?"

He dipped his chin. "Stood outside your hotel room for two hours and couldn't bring myself to knock. I told myself if you wanted me, you'd find me."

I sighed. "I guess you were right about that."

"I knew I would be."

THE BATHROOM'S STEAM CLUNG TO MY SKIN AS I EMERGED FROM the shower and stepped into the open towel Cy held up. He stood there, his gaze unwavering, demanding answers. I felt the weight of my truth bearing down on me, the truth I'd kept hidden for far too long. Facing him, I knew I couldn't hide any longer. I owed him the raw, unfiltered truth that would either mend our fractured past or shatter it irreparably.

And then, as if the weight of those years pressed down on us, he pulled me close once more. His wet chest against mine, our breaths mingling, we clung to each other as if God himself was trying to tear us apart. It was a hug that linked the past and the present, a silent promise that maybe neither of us would let go the second time around. I felt the tremor in his shoulders, the vulnerability he rarely showed, as his thumb gently brushed away a fresh tear.

I eased away from his touch and groaned. "*Fuck*. I can't keep crying like this. I have to pull myself together. He's going to be up soon."

"What's his name?"

"Cree," I answered.

"When's his birthday?"

"Same as yours."

His brows heightened, and his lips curved into a bittersweet smile that held both mercy and disappointment. "Damn. Guess that means you got your hands full, huh?"

I smirked. "Yeah. I do."

He tilted my chin up, forcing me to meet his gaze. "Now that we got that out the way, give me the name of the mothafucka that did this shit to you," he demanded before stripping off his wet clothes and pulling a towel off the rack to dry himself off.

The air in the bathroom thickened as I hesitated, my gaze darting from the towel wrapped around my body to the man who had once been my everything. The silence stretched on, and I wondered how much of my truth I could bear to reveal under his watchful gaze. The last thing I wanted to do was start a war.

My chest deflated with a sigh. "They call him Demon. He's... he's the head of a motorcycle club back where I was staying, the Raging Vipers MC Club.

Cy's jaw clenched. "This the first time this nigga did this shit to you?"

I swung my head in a no as fresh tears blurred my vision. "He's violent, Cy. He's dangerous. But it's not about me anymore."

His anger flared through his nostrils with a hard grunt. "What do you mean?"

"He threatened Cree," I whispered. "Said he'd start taking his anger out on him if I didn't learn how to be a *'good woman.'*"

He flinched as if my words had struck him physically. My eyes met his, raw with pain. One look was all it took for me to see my words had made his blood run cold.

"I grabbed what I could and left in the middle of the night. Once Demon realizes I'm gone, he won't stop until he finds us. I had to come to you, Cy. For Cree's sake, for his protection."

He reached out, his fingers brushing my cheek. "You did the right thing bringing him to me. We'll protect him together," he vowed. "And I promise you, I'll show this Demon mothafucka what it's really like to dance with the devil."

And in that fragile moment, I knew seeing Cy again wasn't just about enlisting his protection for our son. It was about forging new bonds and possibly rekindling old flames.

Chop

A couple of hours later, I stirred from my half-slumber, disoriented by my surroundings. The couch cushions had imprinted on my cheek, and the room was bathed in a bright morning glow. As I rubbed my eyes, the tantalizing aroma of breakfast wafted through the air, pulling me from the clutches of my dream. *Turkey bacon. Freshly scrambled eggs. Pancakes.* My stomach grumbled in response, and I pushed myself up, untangling the throw blanket from my legs. The journey to the kitchen was a blur—a sleepy shuffle across the cold floor, the scent of maple syrup growing stronger with each step.

And there she was: Kendyl, standing at the stove, her melanated silhouette softened by the light. Her hair, once sopping wet, was now bundled in a messy bun with wavy ringlets framing her face. She glanced over her shoulder, and our eyes met—an unspoken understanding passing between us.

She yawned. "I'm sorry. Cree was hungry, and you didn't have any cereal or oatmeal, so I just kind of..."

I shook my head as her sentence trailed off. "You good," I assured her, my voice gravelly from sleep. "Have you slept?"

She slowly wagged her head. "Maybe for about thirty or forty minutes before Cree woke up. I bought myself another thirty minutes of shut eye by offering him his iPad, but of course, he started asking for something to eat."

I broke our gaze and turned to our son. He was huddled on the floor by the fridge, lost in his own little world. My eyes slowly scanned his features, absorbing everything like a sponge now that he was awake and moving around. He was a miniature version of us both. His chubby fingers manipulated two action figures, creating a racket with his imaginary battles. A mop of unruly, dark curls crowned his head, and his chestnut brown eyes were wide and curious. The color was a blend of her gaze and mine. His smile was infectious. It stretched across his innocent face, revealing tiny teeth. When he grinned, I felt the room brighten just a little bit more. His voice was an arrangement of giggles and babbling sentences. He strung words together like beads on a necklace.

When he spotted me, his eyes widened as if he was untangling the world's wonders, one blink at a time. He ran over to Kendyl, clinging to his mother's leg, seeking safety and familiarity. It was the first time he'd met me, and looking into his eyes for the first time would be etched into my memory forever. His gaze flitted between his mother and me, sensing the gravity of our unspoken connection. He didn't understand the complexities yet, but I knew he felt the tension.

"Cree, say hi to mommy's friend," she urged him, her voice gentle but tinged with uncertainty.

My heart clenched at the label. I didn't want to be just a friend; I wanted to be more—a father, a presence in our son's life. I swallowed the lump in my throat, masking my emotions. Kendyl looked at me and mouthed the words *I'm sorry* to me while stirring the lumps out of the batter.

"Hi," he said shyly.

"Wassup, Cree? I'm Cy, but my friends call me Chop."

"Chop like karate?"

I chuckled. "Yeah."

"I like karate."

"Me too, lil man."

I approached Kendyl as she flipped over a golden-brown pancake. We stood there, two adults navigating the delicate road of parenthood. The sizzle of bacon punctuated our conversation as she stepped back to pull the tray out of the oven. Cree stood to the side, watching us with curiosity and caution etched in his expression.

"Cree-Cree, why don't you go back over to your toys? Breakfast is almost ready, okay?"

"Okay, Mommy."

Once he was out of earshot, Kendyl turned to me. "I panicked and didn't want to confuse him," she admitted. "He's still so young. He doesn't know what any of this means. I'm an adult, and I barely know what this means."

"Was he callin' that other nigga you had around him, daddy?"

She swung her head in a no. "No. Never. They only interacted a handful of times over the months we dated. They didn't even meet for the first time until we were four months in. I don't roll like that, Cy. Never have, never will."

I unclenched my fists, relaxing a bit. "I'm sorry. I'd never doubt you being a good mother. I always knew you'd make one."

She scoffed. "Thanks."

"All I'm saying is maybe we can find a better way to introduce me. Something that doesn't diminish my role as his *actual* father, or at least the role I'm trying to have in his life."

"That's fair. Maybe you can read him a bedtime story tonight," she suggested.

A slight smile inched up the right side of my mouth. "That sounds good."

I leaned against the counter, my gaze steady on her beautiful face. The question had been brewing, simmering beneath the surface until it spilled off my lips. "Why Cree?" I questioned, my voice a low murmur. "Why that name for our son?"

She glanced at the stove and then back at me. "It's Native American. I wanted him to carry hope in his name—to rise above our mistakes, our fractured love," she answered, her voice soft as a lullaby.

"I like it," I admitted. And then, as if the words unlocked a hidden door, I continued. "Listen, for now, until we figure all this shit out, I want you to feel comfortable here," I said firmly. "You don't need permission to be a mother. You don't need to apologize for cooking him a meal. No matter how you feel right now, he adores you. I can see how you care for him, the love in his eyes for you."

Her eyes shimmered with tears as she nodded. "Thank you. That means a lot."

"But don't leave. Not yet."

She frowned, confusion etched in her features. "What are you about to do?" she probed, arching a curious brow. "Is it something dangerous?"

I hesitated before revealing the truth. "I'm calling a meeting with The Spades. I need to find out everything I can about the mothafucka you were dating—the one who threatened..."

Her grip tightened around the spatula. "Are you still the... don't tell me, sergeant at arms? Is that what it's called?"

I shook my head. "I'm the new president now since Harlow got killed and Harlan moved to New York," I answered, bringing her up to speed. "And I won't let anyone harm our son."

She nodded hesitantly. "Wow... I guess I owe you a double dose of congratulations."

I shoved my hand in my pocket and retrieved my phone, which had a five percent battery. "Thanks. Yo, put your number in my phone."

She reached out for it before inquiring, "You still got the same number?"

I tipped my head forward in a nod. "Yeah. Never changed it."

"Why not?"

"For you. I figured maybe one day you'd call out of the blue or something."

Kendyl smirked as she passed it back to me. "Except I took it a step further and hunted your ass down at home."

A quick laugh shot through my nostrils. "Right."

"Cree, come to the island and eat. Your breakfast is ready," Kendyl announced before turning her gaze back to me. "You hungry? I made plenty."

"Hell yeah."

"Sit down. I'll make you a plate," she offered.

My hunger gnawed at me, a primal ache that only a hearty breakfast could soothe. As I sat at the kitchen island, two seats down from Cree, the scent of melted butter and warm maple syrup enveloped me. Kendyl moved gracefully between the stove and the countertop, her movements familiar yet distant. The plate before me held a feast: golden pancakes with a generous slab of butter melting into the stack, scrambled eggs, and crispy turkey bacon, just how I liked it. I attacked it with enjoyment, the fork scraping against the empty paper plate. I chewed eagerly—nostalgia and hunger merging.

She glanced at me, her eyes wide as she chuckled. "Slow down, Cy. It's your house. We aren't going to take your food."

I paused, wiping my mouth with the back of my hand. "My bad. I don't know how long it's been since I had a home-cooked meal," I admitted, my voice gruff.

"You're welcome," she said simply. "It's the least I could do."

I nodded, unable to express the tangled emotions—the gratitude, the regret, the longing. I was just glad my ass had opted to go to the grocery store instead of unpacking a few more boxes. I pushed back my chair, scraping against the hardwood floor. "Thanks again. I'll be upstairs. Try to get some rest if you can," I murmured, and she nodded in understanding.

THE MASTER BATHROOM WELCOMED ME—A HAVEN OF STEAM and solitude. The water cascaded from the showerhead, ready to wash away my sins. My mind raced, the droplets echoing my thoughts. I dialed Nitro's number and pressed the phone to my ear. As my new vice president, he answered promptly, the urgency of his voice matching mine.

"Call an emergency meeting at the clubhouse," I informed him.

"What's goin' on?"

"Kendyl's back," I informed him. "Turns out I have a son."

The line went silent for a few fleeting seconds before he mumbled, "Oh shit."

"She's running from a nigga named Cash Majors—the Raging Vipers MC president from the town she was staying in. He threatened her and *our* son."

"Say less. You already know what time it is."

I exhaled, knowing my brothers would rally. They'd ride, fueled by loyalty and wrath. But as the steam filled the bathroom, I whispered one more thing into the phone.

"Have Snake arrange the drive," I instructed. "When they get him, bring his ass straight to me. I'll deal with him for putting bruises on my girl and threatening my son's well-being."

"Bet. We got you," he assured me before ending the call just as my phone died.

I pinned up my long locs before putting my phone on the charger and entering the shower. I watched the running water swirl down the drain as I scrubbed my body from head to toe until I was clean. I stepped out a warrior with a mission. The clubhouse awaited, and deep inside my veins, vengeance simmered.

THE SPADES CLUBHOUSE WAS A RUGGED FORTRESS TUCKED AWAY on the city's outskirts. Its weathered wooden exterior wore the scars of countless storms, both natural and manmade. The neon sign above the entrance flickered, casting an eerie glow on the path leading to the heavy steel door. As I dismounted my motorcycle, the scent of gasoline and burnt rubber hung amongst the idle bikes lining the gravel. The clubhouse was our sanctuary—a place where my leather-clad brothers gathered, our loyalty etched into every square foot.

I trekked inside, eyes catching the long, scarred wooden bar dominating the left side of the room. Bottles of whiskey, cognac, tequila, and moonshine lined the shelves. In the center of the room was a worn pool table awaiting its next game. The dull green felt was pierced with cigarette burns and chalk marks—the residue of countless bets settled over dollars and balls.

Alongside the bar was a trophy wall displaying faded photographs—images of Harlow and Harlan in their prime, their faces defiant and proud as the creators of The Spades. Rally patches, medals, and newspaper clippings told stories of our victories. Upstairs, the heavy door in the back led to my office—the president's office. It was a sacred space where crucial decisions were made. Back downstairs, a small stage occupied the corner, its spotlight dimmed. On weekends, it hosted live bands. It was empty, awaiting the emergency meeting. I strode toward it, my boots echoing on the floor. As the men gathered, their eyes locked onto me. I cleared my throat, and the room fell silent.

"Brothers, we have a situation. Kendyl showed up at my house with my son. She said a man threatened their lives. The mothafucka goes by the name Demon. He's the president of the Raging Vipers. And I don't think I even have to make this clear, but if they weren't our rivals before, they're damn sure about to be."

The room rumbled with anger. "We ride for family," one of the men declared. "That bitch ass nigga's threats won't go unanswered."

My jaw tightened. "When we catch him, we'll bring him here. I'll deal with his ass myself. Show that nigga what we do to mothafuckas that like to beat on women and children."

I may not have been the sergeant at arms anymore, but I was never afraid to put my foot in a nigga's ass, especially one who'd caused harm to someone I loved. In my eyes, that was an act of war. Allegiance ignited around me—a brotherhood bound by blood, leather, and the promise of vengeance. The safety of Kendyl and Cree became the club's sole mission. The Spades MC were about to ride out once more.

Hours later, the clubhouse doors closed behind me, muffling the rumble of the camaraderie of my brothers. The mid-evening air was cool. I pulled out my phone, fingers scrolling through my contacts and stopping at the familiar name that had been etched into my heart since the beginning of time. Kendyl answered on the second ring, her voice calming my restless soul.

"Hey," she said.

"Yo," I replied.

"Everything okay?"

"Y-yeah.

"I was just calling to check in. How are you both?"

"We're good. Cree's down for a nap. I'm just... pacing. It's quiet, and I'm not used to quiet anymore."

I smiled. I could almost see her—standing in the kitchen, the track lights casting shadows on the hardwood floor as she paced from one end to the other. I imagined her hair falling loose and how she bit her lip whenever she was anxious.

"Have you gotten any rest?"

"No. I can't sleep. I'm too anxious. When will you be back?"

My heart clenched. "Soon," I promised. "I need to take care of a few more things first."

"What can I do?" she asked, her voice desperate. "I feel useless here, and I'm going stir crazy."

"Check the pantry, the fridge, and the bathrooms. Make a list of what you think you and Cree will need. Then text it to me. Maybe it'll give you something to do," I suggested.

She hesitated. "You're sure?"

"Yeah. Hit me when you get the list finished."

"Okay. I will."

As I hung up, I revved the engine, allowing the roar to drown out my worries. The road stretched ahead—a path to redemption and another chance at forever with the woman who still had my heart. Fifteen minutes later, I parked my bike at my favorite boxing gym and headed inside. Heavy punching bags hung in the far corner. An elevated professional training ring stood in the center of the floor, its ropes sturdy as two men sparred inside.

I put in my AirPods and tapped shuffle on my workout playlist. "ASAP" by T.I. was up first on the rotation. I approached the punching bag, ready to blow off some steam. I punched harder and harder, imagining it was Demon's face for what he'd put Kendyl through. Had I been there, she *never* would've had to endure that. She would've been safe had she stayed with me. I knew all the what ifs and should've, could've, would've scenarios running through my head were a waste of time and energy. Neither of us could change the past. I wanted to hate her, but every time her beautiful fuckin' face popped up in my head, all I felt was relief that she'd finally come to her senses and come back to a nigga.

My phone vibrated mid-rep, pausing my music. I saw my little sister Nina's name pop up on the screen. Usually, I would've tapped ignore since I was in the middle of my workout, but with everything going on with Kendyl, some part of me craved familiarity.

"Yo," I answered on the third ring.

"Hey, stranger. I can't believe you answered. I almost bet money that you wouldn't."

"Yeah, well, that's because you usually call when I'm in the middle of something important. Like right now."

"What are you doing?"

"I'm working out—blowing off some steam in the gym."

"What's got your feathers ruffled?" she inquired.

I huffed before changing the subject. "How's school?"

"School is school. I'm ready to graduate, I tell you that."

I chuckled. "Yeah. Okay."

She'd always been a brainiac. I wouldn't be surprised if her ass was back in school six months after graduation going back for her master's.

"When's the last time you spoke to Mom and Dad?" she inquired.

I sighed. "It's been a minute. Last Thanksgiving, maybe," I guessed.

"Well, I want to visit my big bro. I miss Chicago. Don't get me wrong, Maryland is cool, but I don't know. There's something special about home."

Nina was ten when my father got a job at the Pentagon. They uprooted from the Chi to the DMV area after I graduated high school. She'd been there for most of her life, so it was natural that she attended college on the East Coast, too.

"I bought a house," I announced.

"You did what?"

"Yeah."

"Congrats! Even more reason for me to come out and see you," she insisted.

It was the second time she'd hinted about coming out to Chicago. "Is there something going on?"

"No. I just miss you."

"I miss you, too, but it isn't a good time right now."

"Why not? What's going on?"

I huffed into the receiver. "I just told you I bought a house. I don't have a bed and barely have any furniture. Give me a few weeks to settle in, and then we can revisit the conversation, all right?"

I decided against telling her about Kendyl's surprise return and the reveal of our son. There were still too many things up in the air for me to feel comfortable talking to her about it. Plus, Nina used to adore Kendyl way back when. There was no way I could bring her up without her asking me a million questions to which I didn't have the answers.

"Okay," Nina agreed.

"Bet. I'll talk to you later. Love you."

"Love you, too," she replied before ending the call.

AFTER LEAVING THE GYM, I HEADED TO THE FURNITURE STORE to pick out new furniture for my home. Then, I went to my old apartment where Mrs. Rodriguez lived. My boots creaked against the worn wooden floor as I approached the stoop—the place Kendyl and I'd once called home. I knocked twice, the sound echoing against the chipped wooden door.

The door swung open, revealing Mrs. Rodriguez—an old woman with silver hair and cocoa-brown eyes that held a lifetime of stories. She was the grandmother of one of The Spades. She'd been living in her house for decades before the bills became too much, and she was forced to move. I had sublet the apartment to her when the new house was almost complete, but I'd never truly left. Not entirely.

I approached her with ease. "Hola, Mrs. Rodriguez," I greeted her. "How's the plumbing holding up? The landlord still giving you issues?"

Her aged bronze face broke into a warm smile. "Ah, mi hijo, it's always something. But you know me—I manage." She dipped her chin as she shuffled aside, silently inviting me in.

I STEPPED OVER THE THRESHOLD, THE SCENT OF AGING WOOD and faded deodorizer enveloping me. The apartment hadn't changed much. Her altar to the Virgin Mary stood in the corner, its flickering candles casting shadows across the carpet. I'd been there a hundred times since Kendyl left, but now that she was back in my life, standing in that apartment had nostalgia tugging at my heart something crazy. Everything seemed to be reminders of a life we'd left behind.

"A girl came by here looking for you. Did she find you?"

I gave her an easy nod. "Yeah. She did."

She lowered her head briefly. "I hope she's okay."

"She is now," I replied, speaking in absolutes.

"Is she your sister?"

"Not quite," I answered, keeping my responses short. I'd only come there for one thing, and one thing only, to check on my stash.

My eyes wandered. I knew every nook and cranny of the place—the creaky, loose floorboard near the kitchen window, the crack in the tile by the bathroom sink. And beneath the floor, hidden from Mrs. Rodriguez's old, prying eyes, lay my secret stash.

I excused myself, claiming I needed to check the fuse box. She nodded, flashing me a smile that reached her sparkling eyes. "Oy vey! Always something."

She inched down the hall as I knelt by the kitchen window overlooking the courtyard. Yellowed lace curtains framed it as dust motes swirled in the air. My calloused fingers traced the edges of the loose floorboard. With practiced ease, I pried it open, revealing a hollow space. There, nestled to the side, were velvet Crown Royal pouches filled with rolls of cash—the blood money from drug deals, bets, and turf wars.

I quickly counted the bills, ensuring they were untouched. The stash had grown over the years, a safety net for when things went south, and now, a start to Cree's college fund. Mrs. Rodriguez had no idea. No one did. To her, this was just an old apartment with creaky floors, faded wallpaper peeling at the edges, and leaky pipes. She deserved peace, and I'd ensure she had it, at least for the next four months left on the lease. I would keep my promise—to fix whatever needed fixing, to look out for her, even if she never knew the extent of my devotion to the apartment.

I closed the floorboard and stood to walk over to the fuse box to check the breakers. For now, the money would stay hidden. I listened to the familiar soft creak of floorboards underfoot as I headed down the hall to find her sitting in her bedroom watching telenovelas.

"Everything okay?" she probed.

"Yes. Everything is okay. Call me or your grandson, Bear, if you need anything, okay?"

"Gracias. I'll see you next time."

I dipped my chin in a firm, decisive nod. "See you."

With one last look around the apartment, I stepped back into the hallway, leaving behind the hidden stash as the door closed softly.

Kendyl

n the cozy embrace of Cy's minimalist kitchen, the air was thick with the intoxicating scent of Italian spices as I stirred in the seasoned spaghetti sauce with the noodles and ground turkey. I sent Cy the list and put in a separate Instacart order for a few items to whip up something quick. I was ready to plate a simple yet soul-soothing plate of spaghetti as soon as he returned. I peeped into the living room at Cree, who was content watching an episode of *Paw Patrol* on his iPad. A smile stretched across my face as the warmth of safety enveloped me like a familiar hug. I hadn't heard from Cash since I blocked his number the night I left. I sent any call from his familiar area code to voicemail just to be safe. I sent resignation emails to both of my jobs, effective immediately. I was about to tell my landlord I'd vacated the property when Remy's call took over the screen.

I took a deep breath and answered. "Hey, Remy," I said, my voice cautious. "What's up?"

"Hey, girl. It's been a couple of days since we last talked. I just wanna make sure you landed on your feet."

I hesitated. I'd be lying to myself if I said fear didn't still cling to me like a shadow. "We're safe," I finally replied. "Cree and I are staying with... an old friend."

"An old friend?" Remy's voice sharpened. "Who?"

"Have you seen him?" I probed, changing the topic. "Y'know, Demon?"

She paused. "No. Has he called you?"

"I wouldn't know. I blocked him."

"Are you sure you're safe?"

I huffed. "I'm sure, Remy, damn."

"Then why can't you tell me where you are or who you're with? You're being so secretive. It's not like you."

"For good reason. You, of all people, know what he put me through."

"And that's exactly why I want to know where you are. I care about you, Kendyl. I swear I'm not trying to be nosey. I'm being a good friend like I've always been. Now, c'mon, you can tell me," she urged.

"Chicago," I admitted. "We're in Chicago."

Silence hung heavy between us as Remy connected the dots. "Wait," she said slowly. "Are you with your *ex*?"

My chest deflated with a sigh. "Yeah," I confessed. "It seemed like the best option, considering I had nowhere else to go."

"Does this mean you two are getting back together?" Remy pressed.

"No," I said firmly. "It's not like that. He's just helping us out."

"So, just so I'm clear," Remy said, frustration creeping into her tone. "You're back with your ex in Chicago?"

"Why are you being so weird about it all?" I shot back. "I'm not committing a crime. He needed to know about our son."

Remy sighed into the receiver. "Okay. You're right," she responded dryly. "As long as you're safe. But promise me you'll be careful."

"I will," the woman replied. "And Remy?"

"Yeah?"

"Don't tell anybody what I just told you, okay?"

She scoffed. "Girl. Who the hell would I even tell?"

"Thanks. I gotta go, all right?"

"Yeah. We'll talk soon."

"Okay," I responded before hanging up.

Twenty minutes later, Cy walked through the front door carrying bags left on the doorstep. It turns out he'd put in a grocery delivery order, too.

"Hey," I greeted him with a half-smile.

"Hey. I hope they got everything you put on your list."

"If not, it's fine. I put in an order for a few things earlier myself. I've got dinner ready on the stove," I told him as we marched into the kitchen.

He rubbed his stomach when he sat the bags on the counter. "It smells good as a mothafucka in here."

We brought all the bags inside from the doorstep and stood side by side at the counter, unpacking them. The clinking of glass jars and tin cans and the rustling of paper bags filled the room as we worked in comfortable silence. I handed him a box of elbow macaroni pasta, and he placed it inside the pantry, our fingers brushing against each other —a fleeting touch that sent a shiver down my spine. *Keep it together, Kendyl. He's already seen you fall apart in front of him once. Don't give him the satisfaction of a second time.*

But then I reached for a can of crushed tomatoes, my fingertips grazing the edge of the shelf. My eyes widened as I realized it was just out of my reach. I looked up at him, my expression mixed with frustration and amusement.

"I can't quite reach," I said, my voice meek.

He stepped behind me without hesitation, his strong hands finding my waist. He lifted me effortlessly, my feet leaving the ground as if they'd gained wings. I gasped, my laughter bubbling up as I placed the can on the top shelf. For a moment, we lingered there, suspended in time—him holding me, me feeling weightless and vulnerable. When he finally set me down, I turned to face him. His brown orbs held a thousand unspoken words. And then, as if drawn by an invisible force, he leaned in, capturing my lips with his. It was a kiss that tasted of nostalgia and longing from all the years we'd spent apart.

As we pulled away, breathless and wide-eyed, he whispered against my lips, "Four years, and I never stopped thinking about you. Wanting you."

His words hung in the air, a fragile bond between our murky past and uncertain future. Before I could respond, Cree burst into the kitchen, his little legs carrying him with the urgency of hunger. His eyes widened at the sight of the spaghetti, and he tugged at my leggings.

"Mommy, I'm hungry!" he declared, his voice a mix of excitement and impatience.

I smiled down at him, my fingers tracing the curve of his tender jaw. "Alright, handsome. Let's get you fed," I declared, ruffling his curls.

Together, the three of us washed up for dinner, Cy and I moving in sync as if muscle memory guided our every step. We sat down at the island with Cree between us, listening to him chatter about his day's adventures and recanting what happened to Chase and Marshall on the latest *Paw Patrol* episode. His words were a delightful jumble of innocence and wonder. I couldn't thank God enough for shielding my son from my mistakes.

And then, just as we were nearing the end of our meal, Cree looked up at his dad. His eyes widened, and he pointed to the birthmark on the inside of Cy's right arm—a small diamond-shaped birthmark etched into his skin.

"You have the same mark as me!" he said, his voice filled with certainty. "Does that mean you're like me?"

The room seemed to freeze in place. Cy glanced over his head at me. My heart galloped. I bit my lip as my gaze searched his face. "Yes," I said softly, my voice barely audible. "Yes, it does."

Cree beamed as if he had just found his new best friend. He reached out to touch the same diamond-shaped birthmark on his neck. "See! See, Mommy! He's like me!"

I sighed. I'd kept my secret for years, shielding our son from the truth. And now, it lay damn near exposed, like an old, tender wound seconds from reopening.

"Cree, why don't you go get your PJs out for bath time," I suggested.

"Okay, Mommy."

When he scampered off, I turned to Cy. My voice trembled. "Y-you don't have to take responsibility," I whispered. "I messed things up by not telling either of you about the other. I understand if you—"

He cut me off, his hand covering mine. "Hell no, Kendyl," he said firmly. "We'll figure this shit out together."

I blinked back tears, my fingers entwining with his. "He needs to know the truth," I declared. "But how do we—"

He leaned in, brushing his lips against mine. "We'll talk about the best way to tell him after we tuck *our* son into bed," he promised.

⁂

AFTER CLEANING THE KITCHEN, I ORCHESTRATED CREE'S nightly bedtime routine, starting with bath time. The bathroom echoed with splashes and giggles as I gently scrubbed away the day's grime. Cree's new rubber duck bobbed in the sudsy water. Cy stood in the doorframe, marveling at how something so simple could bring someone so much joy.

Next came snack time, a delicate balance between nourishment and a treat. I served up apple slices with peanut butter. Cree cheerfully nibbled as he marched around the living room as if it were his own. The real challenge lay in the recurring drinks of water. Cree insisted he was thirsty as if he'd been working in the Sahara Desert all day. His tiny hands gripped the glass as if it held the elixir for eternal life. I patiently encouraged him by saying, "Just a few more sips, Cree Cree," and he begrudgingly complied. Finally, it was time for teeth brushing. I wielded the toothbrush like a magician's wand, charming him into opening his mouth wide. The bubblegum-flavored paste danced across his tiny, gapped teeth, and then we marveled at how his smile sparkled afterward.

"Good job, buddy," I whispered as Cree beamed proudly into Cy's bedroom.

The moonlight scaled higher in the dark sky, revealing a silver glow through the window. The three of us gathered around his box spring and mattress combo. The room was hushed as Cree, clothed in his favorite dinosaur pajamas, wiggled underneath the covers. His eyes were heavy with sleep, but he fought to stay awake.

"Mommy, tell me a story," he whispered, his voice a soft request.

"Actually, I was thinking..."

Cy cut me off again. "What do you say we give your mom a break, and you let me read you a story tonight, lil man?" he proposed to Cree.

A wide-gapped smile spread across his little face as he nodded in agreement. Cy sat on the edge of the mattress, brushing a ringlet of unruly hair from Cree's forehead.

"Aight, bet," he began. "Once upon a time, there was a brave knight named, uh, uh, Leo. He lived in this dope magical kingdom where fire-breathing dragons roamed the forests, and tiny fairies danced in the flowers."

I sat beside them, my fingers tracing comforting circles on Cree's back. "And Leo had a secret," I added, my voice conspirative. "He had a birthmark shaped like a diamond on his arm—a mark that connected him to someone very special."

Cree's eyes widened. "Who?" he asked, his curiosity piqued.

Cy and I exchanged glances. "Someone you just met who already loves you very much," he answered him.

Cree yawned, snuggling deeper into the blankets. "Is it Mommy?" he mumbled, his words slurred with sleep.

My heart clenched. "Yes," I whispered. "It's Mommy."

Cy leaned down, pressing a kiss to Cree's forehead. "And it's me too," he said. "We're a family, lil man."

Cree's eyelids drooped. "Family," he echoed, his voice fading.

"Sleep tight, my little prince," I whispered before kissing his forehead.

We tucked him in, and I turned off the bedside lamp, leaving only the moonlight to guide us back out into the hall. Cy lingered, his hand resting on the doorknob for a bit before we tiptoed down the hall, leaving our son wrapped in the safety of his sweet dreams.

When the house was calm, he turned to me, eyes searching mine, before he asked, "Is it this exhausting every night?" His voice was marked with weariness and wonder.

I smiled. "Not every night," I confessed. "Some nights, I read him *six* bedtime stories. And occasionally, I have to bribe him with an extra snack, which means brushing his teeth twice."

"Damn."

Our laughter filled the living room, a melody that chased away the day's uncertainties. "Oh, the sweet exhaustion that comes with being a parent."

He ran his hands over his fuzzy locs. "I've got a lot to learn."

"Don't worry. With enough practice, you'll catch on to it all someday."

Chop

Kendyl and I re-entered the living room. The cushions on my new leather couch creaked as we settled onto it.

I broke the silence. "That lil alley-oop you did with the bedtime story back there was cool and all, but I want to be a part of his life in a real way," I said, my voice raw. "Our son deserves to know me—to know about us."

Kendyl shifted, her fingers tracing the edge of the couch. "What will it mean for him?" she asked softly. "To know you're his father?"

My gaze held hers. "I don't know," I admitted. "But I want to find out. I want to be there for him—to watch him grow up, to share in his laughter and tears. I've already missed out on his first three years. I can't imagine missing out on anymore."

She nodded. "Okay. We'll talk to him tomorrow and tell him about us. About everything."

"And what about us?" I quizzed. "Are we going to try and be together again?"

She hesitated, then shook her head. "Maybe that's not the answer," she said. "Maybe we've both changed too much."

"Then what about custody?" I pressed. "What happens when you move out? Will we split holidays and weekends?"

Kendyl's chest deflated with a hard sigh. "I haven't thought any of this shit through, Cy. None of it," she confessed. "But I know I don't want the courts involved. I want to do the right thing—for him."

I leaned back, staring at the ceiling. "We'll figure it out," I said finally. "As time goes by."

She turned to me, her eyes soft. "For now, I want you to spend as much time with him as you want."

"Oh, I was doin' that regardless," I assured her.

"Thank you for wanting to be a father to our son. I know there are a lot of men who wouldn't have been so graceful about stepping up to the plate like you have."

"Thank you for finally giving me the chance."

I pulled her closer to my side of the couch before setting her on my lap. Kendyl nestled her head underneath my neck while I cradled her like a baby. And then, our lips met—the sweet taste of understanding lingering. My heart, like a resting ember, flared to life. The ache of missed chances and lost time fueled me. I craved more—all of her, an opportunity to give our wild love story a new ending. As we pulled away, our eyes met. And in that gaze, I saw reflections of our past selves—the young couple who once believed in spending a couple of forever's together.

"What now?" I murmured, the rumble of my voice barely audible.

She leaned closer, her lips brushing my ear. "I'm not ready to get my heart broken again," she whispered, her voice trembling.

I cupped her face in my hands, my eyes trained on hers. "You can trust me," I promised, my words a solemn vow. "With your life and your heart."

"As much as I want to believe you—"

As her sentence faded, my fingers found hers. She didn't pull away. "We'll take shit as slow as you want," I told her, voice steady.

"Okay," she murmured, her fingers entwined with mine.

"One step at a time."

She nodded, her fingers tracing the edge of my jaw. "No rushing," she agreed. "No diving headfirst."

"But I'd be lying if I said I didn't want to show you how much a nigga missed you."

Passion surged through us like a wildfire consuming us whole. Our hands found their way under each other's clothes, yearning for skin-to-skin contact. I kissed down her tatted shoulders, pulling her tank top over her headful of curls before my lips devoured hers again. She lifted my shirt over my head before I laid her back against the couch, making out like a couple of sex-crazed teens. My hands explored every inch of her body, relearning the contours, the taste, the rhythm.

I unhooked her bra and scattered a trail of kisses down her chest. My tongue swirled around her chocolate nipples, firm and sweet like two Hershey's Kisses. I pulled down her shorts and panties before continuing my trail of kisses down to her belly button.

"We have to be quiet," she whispered. "I don't want to wake up Cree."

I climbed on top of her, parting her legs before diving between her soft thighs. "I suggest you put your hand over your mouth or bite down on something because nothings gonna stop me from fucking the shit out of you tonight, Kendyl."

Kendyl lay parallel against the couch, hands roaming across my exposed muscles as my tongue recited all the words I'd never said against her soft folds. She still tasted like brown sugar and pineapples.

"Ooooh shit," she purred, locking her thighs around my neck.

I licked Kendyl's pussy from A to Z, forward and backward, making up for as much lost time as possible. I flashed my eyes up at her, admiring the arch in her back and how she squirmed under my tongue's command. After I made sure she was nice and wet, I sat up and pulled down my basketball shorts and boxers to my ankles.

Kendyl straddled me, flipping her curls out of her face as she eased down onto my rod.

She gasped. "Oooh fuck." Her eyes were wide, her heart beating rapidly through her chest.

Our lips were like magnets, drawn to each other. Each kiss felt like a declaration—a tribute to the spark that had never truly died between us. My hands moved about her body gently as if cradling a delicate dove. I held her close to me as she slowly popped up and down.

The echoes of heavy breathing filled the room. "Fuck, Cy. You feel so good," she whispered through her moans.

Her lips found mine again—the safest way to stifle her pleasure. As she picked up the pace, I gripped her nape and slammed her down on top of me. I wanted her to feel every inch she'd been missing. My hands gripped her petite waist, taking turns smacking her jiggling ass as she rode me like a bucking bronco, relieving her stress. She grabbed the leather couch, grinding harder into me. Our bodies were saying all the words our mouths couldn't.

My fingertips were lost in a sea full of her curls. "Goddamn, I fuckin' missed you," I growled.

I rose from the couch, hands palming her ass as I fucked her standing up. The light from the TV illuminated her body as I eased her up and down my rod. Regret danced on the edges of each hard thrust—the missed anniversaries, the unspoken apologies, the love left unexplored.

Switching positions, I eased her back to her feet and bent her petite frame over the couch to beat the pussy up from behind. The locket around my neck swung forward with each stroke, smacking against my chest. I reached around to strum her clit with precision as if I were the lead guitarist in a rock band. I replaced my dick with my finger and finger fucked her until she squirted.

Kendyl's nails dug into the leather, gripping onto the couch for dear life. "Ooooh fuck! Fuck! Yes! Just like that!" she squealed.

I slid back inside her, swiping my locs out of my face before bending forward to kiss down the back of her shoulders and the top of her spine. I panted heavily in her ear as she bounced back against me.

"That's it, baby. Show me how much you missed this fuckin' dick."

My fingertips skated down her spine before I smacked her ass. I spread her cheeks to ensure she was getting every inch of me. A devilish smirk spread across my face when I saw how white she'd turned my dick from cumming.

"Oh my God!"

I yanked her hair back to see her beautiful brown orbs rolling back in her head. "Take this dick. Take all this dick. It's all yours, Kendyl."

Kendyl moaned. "I'm cumming again, Cy! I'm fucking cumming!"

Our hearts beat in sync as we lay back on the couch, side by side. My dick was buried deep inside her, whispering promises to her body with each stroke. The future was uncertain, but for now, I planned to savor every moment she was in my presence.

I held Kendyl tight, digging into her. My lips brushed against her neck. "Fuck. I'm about to nut," I groaned, thrusting harder.

As I succumbed to the feeling of euphoria, I pulled out and busted my nut down the back of her thigh as we kissed.

Kendyl

I stirred on the couch hours later, my eyes fluttering open. The room was hushed, the air cool against my skin. I shifted, my fingers brushing against the warmth of Cy's ink-stained arm. He slept soundly, his breaths steady and rhythmic. Four years apart, and yet there we were, tangled in the delicate web of intimacy. I was like a moth to an old flame. The warmth of his skin against mine and the feeling of him deep inside me had ignited stifled embers, and now I stood at the crossroads of possibility.

Hope fluttered in my chest, foolishly whispering promises of second chances. After all, he still looked at me as if I held the universe in my eyes. Yet caution murmured, too. Fear tiptoed along the edges of my desire. What if our reconnection was a fragile illusion conjured by the moonlight and nostalgia? What if we shattered each other's hearts all over again, this time with our son hanging in the balance? I'd learned the hard way that love wasn't always enough. The weight of my uncertainty seemed to lift as I eased myself up, careful not to wake him.

The carpeted stairs creaked under my weight as I ascended. I paused outside the bedroom door, my hand resting on the fresh wood.

Inside, Cree lay cocooned under the covers, his adorable face peaceful in slumber. His chest rose and fell with each fleeting breath. I smiled, my heart swelling with love. A calming feeling washed over me for a few fleeting minutes, making me believe everything would be alright. The doubts, the fears—they melted away in the softness of that room.

I slipped into the bed beside him, my body fitting perfectly against his. His warmth seeped into my bones, chasing away the chill of uncertainty that lingered between his father and me. *Don't put all your eggs in one basket, Kendyl.* Was it reckless to hope to be more than Cree's parents? To believe that we could forget the past and build something more substantial the second time around? Did we owe it to our son to try, or were we better off trying to be friends? Over the years, I'd become good at self-preservation, guarding my heart behind walls of independence. But being with Cy again and under his protection made me feel different.

As I closed my eyes, I imagined a future where Cy would continue to rise to the occasion for our son. He'd be the man who would be there, not just in my time of need, but consistently—a steady presence in Cree's life—*our* lives. I believed in the goodness within him, the immense potential waiting to be unlocked as he navigated fatherhood. Maybe I was dick dizzy or simply being naive, but just like a good dick down, hope had a way of blurring the edges of reality. Nevertheless, the weightlessness was intoxicating—a rare pardon from my daily burdens. I happily drifted into sleep with a smile lingering on my lips.

THE MORNING SUN BEAMED THROUGH THE KITCHEN WINDOW, casting extended shadows on the hardwood floor. The fragments of intimacy clung to my skin as I reread Cy's text, the words etching themselves in the pit of my stomach: *Home late. Don't wait up.* The knot in my stomach tightened. *Is this regret? Or merely convenience?*

I'd expected to wake up and see him still sleeping soundly on the couch or maybe even taking a shower. I hadn't expected to wake up to a house with only Cree and me and a cryptic text.

Cy's absence echoed through the house, a hollow ache that threatened to swallow me whole. I imagined him out there—perhaps drowning his doubts in the neon glow of the clubhouse or maybe roaming the streets on his bike, wrestling with demons I couldn't begin to comprehend. *Is he avoiding me? Why did he slip away like smoke through my fingers?*

As I poured cereal into Cree's bowl, my mind churned. Optimism and doubt danced their age-old waltz. Maybe he needed some space—time to sort through the tangled web of our past. Or perhaps he regretted taking things further than we said we would—how our bodies had sought solace in each other's warmth. And then the doorbell shattered my trance. Without hesitation, I crossed the room, my heart fluttering like a tiny bird. I swung the door open, expecting to find a solicitor or a delivery person. But the man standing on the threshold was neither. His eyes bore into mine—dirt brown, like specks of mud. Recognition slammed into my chest, stealing my breath away.

Cash stood there. His presence was a nightmare, a cruel twist of fate piercing my safety bubble. He looked me up and down, assessing my vulnerability—the way a predator sizes up its prey. I had no weapon, no protection, no chance. His grip on my arm felt like a hot brand against my skin.

"Pack your shit, *bitch*," he commanded, his voice a venomous whisper. "You two are coming with me."

Fear clawed at my throat. I glanced back at the stairs, wishing Cree was still asleep and blissfully unaware. I couldn't believe Demon—a coldhearted monster, had found us. The fragile cocoon of hope I'd gotten comfortable in hours before shattered, leaving only shards of desperation. I'd escaped him once. Could I do it again?

Chop

The bustling airport hummed with life as travelers hurried past, their footsteps echoing against the polished floors. I stood near the baggage claim carousel, my eyes scanning the crowd for Harlan. We hadn't seen each other in a few months since Clover had given birth to their daughter, Brave. Finally, Harlan emerged from the crowd, wheeling a suitcase behind him. His eyes lit up when he spotted me, and we embraced like old homies do. I immediately noticed the tired lines etched around his eyes—the weariness of travel mixed with the newness of fatherhood.

"Man, it's been too long," Harlan said, clapping me on the back. "Thanks for picking me up."

"No problem," I replied.

"So, what's been up with you lately, nigga? Catch me up."

I hesitated, then grinned. "Fatherhood, my nigga. I'm a dad now."

Harlan raised an eyebrow. "*You*? A dad? When the fuck did that happen, and who the fuck did you knock up?"

My eyes softened. "That's the crazy part. It turns out that when Kendyl left, she was pregnant. She never told me I had a kid out there until she fuckin' showed up on my doorstep a couple of days ago. I never thought I'd be a father, but just looking at him... I don't know. A part of me wants to hate Kendyl for what she did, but every time I look at him, all I can be is grateful to her for having him in the first place."

Harlan shot me a dazed look while jerking his head back in surprise. "Damn. This shit is wild, bro. I leave the fuckin' city, and your entire life blows up."

"Hell yeah. This shit is the wildest thing that's ever happened to me, bruh, like forreal. And you know I've seen some shit and done some shit too."

"What's his name? You got a picture of lil man?" Harlan inquired.

I swung my head in a no. "His name is Cree. And nah. I haven't had the chance to snap anything. Whenever I'm with him, I'm just in the moment, you know? Soaking up everything I can about him while he's here."

"I feel that. That's how I felt when Brave was born."

"How's Clover doing? You said she had a C-section, right?"

"Yeah. She's good. Everything is healing how it's supposed to, and they're both here healthy and happy. That's all I can ask for."

"That's wassup. So what's next for you two?" I inquired. "Do a nigga hear wedding bells anytime soon? Just let me know ahead of time because you know a nigga looks good in a custom-fitted tux," I joked.

Harlan's shoulders bobbed as he pulled out his phone. He silently scrolled through it before flashing his screen at me. On it was a picture of a diamond engagement ring. "I got it at the crib. I just haven't figured out when I wanna ask her yet," he stated.

My eyes widened as we neared my car. "Oh shit. Congratulations, bruh."

He cheesed. "Thank you. What about you? Everybody doesn't get a second chance with the one that got away."

I shook my head before ducking into the driver's seat. "I don't know, man. Shit is all kinds of fucked up right now. We said we're taking shit slow, but we still really ain't got to the meat of it all yet."

"You love her, don't you?" Harlan asked as he fastened his seat belt.

I sucked my teeth before darting a knowing glare at him. "You know I do, nigga."

"Then don't let her get away again. That's all I'm saying."

"It's not that simple," I explained, pulling onto the highway.

"Why not? She's back in your life for a reason, ain't she?"

"She's on the run from her ex, some nigga named Demon."

"From the Raging Vipers MC Club?"

"Yeah. You heard of 'em?"

"He and Low had words at a car meet a long ass time ago. I don't fuck with his ass. That's for sure."

"Yeah, well, the nigga bruised her up and threatened to harm my son."

Harlan's nostrils flared. "Oh, hell no. That mothafucka must got a death wish! Why the fuck didn't you tell me this shit sooner?" Harlan roared.

"Because I know you got a lot on your plate right now with the new baby and shit. I wasn't trying to burden you with more stress, especially when it's my responsibility. I'm the president of The Spades now. I gotta handle this shit my way."

Before he could respond, my phone rang. "Wassup, Nitro?" I answered as the loud roaring of engines in his background blared through my car speakers.

"Demon and a couple of riders from his crew are in town," he stated, his voice direct.

I gripped the steering wheel, and my tatted knuckles hardened. "What? Where is he?"

"I don't know just yet. I've got riders out all over the city looking for him now. When I know something, you'll be the first person I call."

I ended the call as my foot mashed against the gas pedal. The city's neon lights blurred into streaks as I weaved through traffic, adrenaline pumping.

"Chop!" Harlan shouted, his jaw set. "What the fuck is going on?"

My jaw clenched. "He's here for her. I know he is. This isn't a friendly visit, nigga. It's a declaration of fuckin' war."

Harlan's eyes widened before darkening. "You strapped?"

I smirked with a nod. You could take the nigga out the Chi, but you couldn't take the Chi out the nigga. Before I could respond, my phone buzzed. I glanced at the screen, and my expression darkened.

I answered, my voice low and dangerous. "Where is he?"

"We spotted him heading toward the interstate," he muttered. "They've got your son and his mother."

"Man, fuck!" I roared. "Stay on his tail, and do *not* fuckin' lose them!" I ordered before the call ended.

"We'll get them back," Harlan said, trying to steady his nerves.

My grip on the wheel tightened even more as rage bubbled up inside me. I felt like I could Hulk out and yank it right out of the steering column. "How the fuck did he find her? I should've protected them. I never should've left them alone. I should've been there."

"You can't blame yourself," he insisted. "You didn't know."

"But I'm his fuckin' father!" I spat. "I was supposed to protect them! I got too comfortable. I should've brought them to the clubhouse where they would've been protected twenty-four-seven!"

As we sped toward the clubhouse on the outskirts of town, Harlan reached for my shoulder. "Listen, we'll strategize. We'll get your son *and* Kendyl back. But right now, you need to focus, nigga. Anger won't help. Stay calm. Stay focused."

I nodded to his words, knowing that calm was a distant memory. By the time I was done with Demon, he was going to be *begging* for me to drag his ass back to hell.

Kendyl

My small apartment felt even smaller as the door slammed shut, trapping Cree and me in a waking nightmare. Demon's rugged grip on my arm was like a vise, and I winced as he dragged me inside. Cree, wide-eyed and trembling, clung to my leg.

"Baby boy, go to your room," I instructed him, my voice barely audible. "Hide in your favorite spot. Don't come out until mommy finds you, okay? You'll be safe there."

He nodded, his big eyes filling with fear. He hurried down the hallway, disappearing into the safety of his hiding place—a closet filled with the stuffed animals, clothes, and blankets we'd left behind. My heart ached as I watched him go, knowing I had to protect him at all costs. I twisted my neck toward the gaping front door when I heard a familiar voice. I was surprised to see Remy standing there. Remy, the friend I'd trusted, had betrayed me. I'd spent the entire six-and-a-half-hour drive retracing my steps, trying to figure out how he'd managed to find me, and it had been her ass all along. My anger simmered beneath the surface, but my fear of Demon's retaliation kept my lips buttoned tight.

Remy's tearful eyes met mine. "Kendyl, I'm *so* sorry," she whispered.

"*You*," I spat at Remy, my voice low and nasty as a vengeful tear slipped down my cheek. "You told him where to find me after you said you wouldn't tell anyone!"

"He threatened my kids, just like he threatened your son! Said he'd hurt them if I didn't help him track you down."

My mind raced. I didn't know what to believe. Remy had been my lifeline, who had kept me sane during the long drive to Chicago and watched Cree for me on my long nights at the bar. But now, that trust was shattered.

"You fucking sold me out," I accused.

"I had no choice," Remy pleaded. "I thought... I thought he'd just talk to you. I didn't know he'd drag you back here like this."

Demon stepped between us, smirking at the satisfaction of being the one who'd been pulling the strings all along. "You can't run forever," he warned, cracking his knuckles. "Not from me, baby."

I clenched my fists, bracing myself for a struggle. Remy's betrayal cut deep, but I also knew that people would go to great lengths for the ones they loved, even if it meant sacrificing someone else.

"Go the fuck home, bitch. Your services are no longer needed," Demon spat toward Remy with a grimace etched on his brow.

Remy stumbled backward over the threshold before freezing in place and whispering the two words that let me know her chosen side. "*I'm sorry.*"

I blinked as the apartment door slammed shut behind her, and the back of Demon's hand collided with my face with a hard *thwap*. His violent advance caught me off guard, knocking me to the ground with minimal effort. His size ten-and-a-half boot connected with my side the minute I hit the floor.

"Ahhhh!" I screamed out in pain, gripping my ribs to protect them from another potential blow.

Demon, the dark side of the man who'd tormented me for far too long, stood over me with a twisted smile on his lips. "*Nobody* fuckin' leaves me twice," he hissed, the words dripping with malice. "You'll learn that tonight. Then, when I'm done with you, I'm gonna go into that back room, find your little brat, and beat the shit out of him, too. Maybe then you'll think twice about running into another nigga's arms and giving away what's mine."

I lay crumpled on the floor, tears streaming down my tender cheek. I glanced over my shoulder, fear gripping me as my eyes spotted his gun on the kitchen counter. Demon had carelessly left it there in his rage.

"P-please just l-leave him alone," I whispered as I slowly climbed to my feet.

"You know, when you ran off like that, I sent men scouring all over the city for you. And then I said, hm, it's time to work smarter and not harder. So, I ran down on Remy and asked her about you. That bitch started hemming and hawing. It wasn't until I put a gun to that ho's skull and threatened to blow her brains out that she mentioned you two used to share locations. Turns out, you never turned it off. I made her call you to check, and when you said Chicago, that gave me all the information I needed."

I winced, drawing in a deep breath. *Fuck.* I'd shared my location with her on nights that I had her watch Cree for me, just so she knew I was all right, and in the midst of all the chaos, had forgotten to turn it off. Demon advanced toward me, rage burned in his eyes, ready to strike me again. I made a split-second decision. Instead of waiting for him to attack me, I lunged at him first, ignoring the pain in my ribs from our initial scuffle. We grappled, crashing into furniture and sending a lamp crashing to the ground before we stumbled toward the kitchen. *C'mon, Kendyl. All you have to do is get close enough to the gun.* My heart pounded as we reached the counter. I drew my leg back and kicked Demon as hard as I could in the balls, sending him to his knees. I twisted my neck. There it was—the gun. In a split second, my fingers closed around the cold metal, and I turned to face the shell of a man who'd haunted my life.

My voice was steady, although my body shook. "This shit ends now," I whispered. "Do you fuckin' hear me? Nobody gets hurt by you again!"

His eyes widened with disbelief etched across his face. The tension in the kitchen was thick and suffocating. My grip on the gun tightened as I stepped in front of Demon, who was frozen. As shook as he looked, he was not about to let me see him sweat.

"Put the fuckin' gun down, Kendyl," he spat, his voice a low growl as he slowly started to climb to his feet. "We both know you don't have the fuckin' guts to use it."

My thoughts raced. I had to protect myself and my son, but he was right. I couldn't pull the trigger. Not with Cree down the hall. Not in cold blood. I shook my head, swallowing the melon-sized lump in my throat. My heart pounded, adrenaline surging through my veins as my finger hovered over the trigger. I remembered the countless nights of fear, the bruises, the broken promises. I remembered my tears, my recurring dreams of escape. There was no other choice. I *had* to end my nightmare.

Demon's face twisted into a demonic snarl. "You think you're clever, don't you, bitch?" he sneered. "But you're both dead. I already told you, no one leaves me. Now put the fuckin' gun down, Kendyl! Last chance, bitch," he spat, quickly lunging forward.

My finger squeezed the trigger, and the gunshot echoed through the small kitchen. Time seemed to slow to a crawl as Demon staggered back, crimson blood blossoming on his chest. His eyes widened in shock before he crumpled to the floor. I stood there, trembling, the weight of Demon's gun still warm in my palm. His body lay sprawled on the floor, lifeless. *It was self-defense.* It was a desperate act to escape months of torment he'd inflicted upon me and any future torment for my son. I shot a panicked look toward the front door as it creaked open, revealing Remy. Our eyes locked. Her shock mirrored mine. She'd heard the struggle and stood as the sole witness to my crime. *It was self-defense.*

"What..." Remy's voice cracked. "Kendyl, what the fuck happened?"

I couldn't afford to hesitate. "He attacked me," I whispered, my voice stripped of emotion. "I had no choice."

Remy's wide-eyed gaze shifted from me to Demon's body. "Self-defense," she murmured as if convincing herself. "They'll believe you."

I hesitated. Would they? I'd endured months of bruises and assumed threats. Yet, I'd never officially gone on the record about any of it. My heart pounded. If I made the call, what would come next? The police? A mountain of questions I didn't have the answers to? I'd seen enough crime shows and thriller movies to know the drill, but the reality was a vast difference. My hands trembled as I slowly placed the gun back on the kitchen counter, careful not to disturb the evidence.

She inched closer to me. "Kendyl, snap out of it! There's a dead body in the middle of your kitchen, and your son is in the next room. You *need* to call the cops," Remy urged, her voice steadier.

Chop

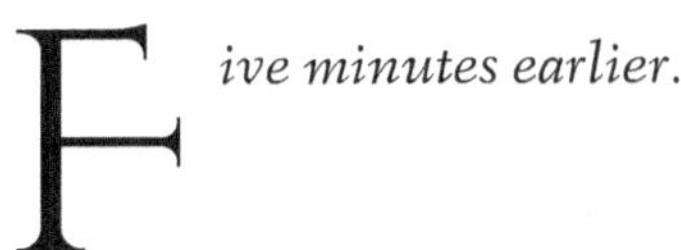

THE NIGHT AIR WAS THICK WITH TENSION AS I SPED DOWN THE dimly lit streets, following the GPS to Demon's last traceable where-abouts. My heart pounded as the engine drowned out my thoughts. Harlan sat to my right in the passenger seat, strapped with a bullet-proof vest and a gun. I tried my best to stay focused and not assume the worst, but we and the riders to the front and back were prepared for whatever.

As I pulled up to the apartment building my men had tracked them to, the sound of a gunshot echoed through the night. Without hesitation, I parked and exited the running car, adrenaline surging. I kicked open the door, my leather boots crashing against the wood. The scene before me was a nightmare etched in crimson. Kendyl and a woman I'd never seen before stood on the linoleum floor. Demon lay sprawled nearby with blood soaked through his shirt. The gun lay on the counter as the kitchen light illuminated Kendyl's tear-streaked face. I drew my weapon, aiming it at the woman while keeping my eyes trained on Kendyl.

"Are you hurt?" I rasped, my voice gruff.

Kendyl shook her head, her eyes wide. "No, just scared."

The woman spoke up. "She was just about to call the cops."

"Nobody's callin' anybody. Now move," I ordered, waving her to the side with my gun. "Kendyl, who the fuck is she, and where's Cree?"

"She's my neighbor, Remy. And Cree, h-he's hiding in his room."

"What about that nigga? Is he dead?"

She nodded. "It was self-defense."

"And the police will understand," Remy added.

"Bitch, shut the fuck up!" I roared, releasing the safety. "Like I said, nobody's callin' the fuckin' cops."

The woman's eyes widened. "Wait. W-what are you doing?"

"Chop, don't," Kendyl asserted, calling me by my road name.

I cut my eyes at her and shook my head. "Do you trust her?"

"Cy, I—"

"Do you fuckin' trust this bitch, Kendyl?" I challenged again.

She hesitated, and I pulled the trigger, sending a bullet into the center of her forehead. Once Remy's lifeless body hit the floor, I turned to Kendyl and saw a tear slip down her face. "It was our family or hers. Don't shed a tear. It wasn't your decision to make."

She'd done what she had to—defended herself and our son, and I'd come in to ensure her secrets stayed just that. I didn't know her neighbor from Adam, but she was talking too much about the police, which meant she was quick to flip. My eyes locked onto hers.

"S-she kept urging me to call the police and tell them everything. She insisted they'd understand. But I—I didn't trust her, Cy. Not after finding out she was the one who told Demon where I was," her voice wavered as she recounted the events.

I rushed to her side and scooped her up. Her fragile frame fit perfectly against my chest. I smelled the fear and desperation clinging to her skin. Her tears flowed freely—relief, grief, and possibly a strange mix of guilt. She'd taken a life and lost a neighbor in the process, but it was she who'd survived. Her chest heaved, and she pushed herself away from me.

"Cree—"

Before finishing, she broke free from my arms and sprinted toward the first bedroom. I followed, my heart pounding. She knelt by the closet in the small room, pulling the door open. Cree huddled inside, clutching his teddy bear, his eyes wide with terror. My chest tightened. My son was safe, but the trauma etched on the boy's face would haunt me forever.

"Mommy? Is the bad man gone?" his tiny voice called out.

Kendyl raced to him, gathering Cree into her trembling arms and whispering soothing words. "It's okay, baby. Mommies got you. You're safe now."

I watched, feeling a tornado of emotions. I'd seen too much violence, too many lives shattered. But this—this was different. Kendyl had fought back and gone to great lengths to protect our son. She'd become a warrior in her own right. As much as I hated interrupting the moment, we had important shit to handle. I stepped away and texted Harlan, who'd been waiting downstairs, monitoring the area with the other riders. Within seconds, The Spades rushed in, removing the two dead bodies from the apartment and erasing any sign of a struggle.

I waved Kendyl over to the doorway of Cree's old bedroom. "Did you touch anything besides the gun?" She swiftly shook her head, eyes frozen on the floor. "Strip," I announced, snapping her back to the present.

She shifted her focus up to me. "*What?*"

"Take off your clothes right now. We gotta get rid of all the evidence," I informed her before closing her inside Cree's room.

When we emerged from the apartment, I carried Cree, and Kendyl clung to my side. Outside, sirens wailed in the distance, growing louder as the seconds passed. The longer we stayed, the more I knew we'd risk facing the consequences—the police, the questions. We had to get the hell out of there.

The night air was cool against our skin as I put Cree and Kendyl in the back seat of my car. Harlan sat behind the wheel, giving me a break from driving back to Chicago with no questions asked.

Before I closed the door, Cree's small voice broke the silence. "Mommy, where are we going?"

My gaze met Kendyl's, determination burning in my eyes. "We're going home, lil man," I answered, my voice steady.

She agreed with a nod. "That's right. We're going home."

Kendyl

The first light of dawn painted the sky in yellow, red, and orange hues. Cree and I exited the car, stretching our tired limbs after the long six-and-a-half-hour drive. The early morning air was crisp, guaranteeing a new day—a fresh start after all the darkness. As we approached the front door, my exhaustion weighed heavily on me. I'd been riding for hours, trying to keep myself from falling apart in the back seat, my eyes heavy with fatigue and guilt. Cy placed a gentle hand on my shoulder, and I flinched.

"Listen, I know you're tired," he said softly. "But I have a surprise for both of you."

Curiosity piqued as I exchanged a glance with Cree. He was still half-asleep, clinging to my hand. We followed Cy inside, the hardwood floor creaking beneath our feet. Upstairs, the hallway was dim, but a soft glow emerged from the first room. Cy pushed open the door, revealing a sight that took my breath away. The budding sunlight bathed the room, glistening across the brand-new furniture. Against one wall stood a toddler bed with neutral sheets and a plush dinosaur pillow. A tiny wooden chair and table set stood by the window.

"This is his room," Cy announced, his voice filled with pride. "His very own space."

I inched inside with my free hand cupped over my mouth in surprise. "But h-how did you manage to—"

"You'd be surprised what a nigga can make happen in a little over twelve hours."

"But... how'd you know th–that we'd make it back?"

"I wasn't leaving without either of you, Kendyl. I put that on my life."

Tears welled up in my eyes. I'd never expected it. Cree rubbed his eyes while shuffling over to the bed and climbing onto it. His bubbly giggles filled the room as he bounced up and down, awakening his tired limbs. I sank onto the chair, overwhelmed with gratitude. It was a sweet ending to such a sour night.

"Thank you," I whispered, my voice catching. "Thank you for giving him this."

Cy knelt beside me, taking my hand. "He deserves it," he said. "And so do you."

As the sun continued to rise, stretching its golden rays through the window curtains, I realized the moment was bigger than new furniture. It was about his love, sacrifice, and the promise of a brighter future as a family. I reached out and hugged Cy tightly, feeling the warmth of our small family enveloped in the room. His surprise was the most beautiful gift I'd ever received—a bedroom for Cree inside a home filled with love and promise.

AFTER WASHING CREE UP AND PUTTING ON HIS PJs, I GENTLY laid him in his new toddler bed, tucking the soft blankets around him. The room was cozy. I looked around at the bare walls and thought about painting them a soothing shade of blue. No sooner than the thought crossed my mind, flashbacks of Demon and Remy's dead bodies appeared in my head. The memory of his rage, our desperate struggle, and the final act that had saved our lives—it all played on a loop in my mind.

Feeling the weight of the day, I stood in the doorway, watching Cree with a ghost of a smile. He yawned, his eyelids drooping, and soon he was fast asleep. I tip-toed out of the room, leaving the door slightly ajar. I needed a moment to myself. The adrenaline from our traumatic escape still pulsed through my veins.

Inside the master bathroom, I turned on the shower, warm steam, and the sound of water filled the space. I sat on the edge of the toilet, my trembling hands resting on my knees. The adrenaline began to fade, leaving me feeling drained and raw. The reality of what I'd done and what I'd witnessed hit me like a tidal wave. I knew I'd taken a life in self-defense, and I knew Remy was no good for what she did to me, but the weight of it settled heavily on my chest, making it hard to breathe. She had kids. What would happen to them? *If Cy hadn't gotten to her, it probably would've only been a matter of time before Demon's crew did.* I understood the rules of survival enough to know that it had to be her or me. It couldn't be both of us.

As the warm water flowed in the shower, I stripped down and stepped inside. Then the sobs came, uncontrollable and fierce. I clung to the tiled wall. My legs felt weak and threatened to give way. The guilt, the fear, the trauma—it all flooded over me like a tsunami. It felt like I'd been hit by a Mack truck, both emotionally and physically.

Through my sobs, I heard the bathroom door creak open, and the shower curtain slightly pull back. Cy stood there with concern etched in his features. He'd heard my cries. Without a word, he kept his eyes pinned on me as he gently eased the curtain back into place before standing guard in front of the shower. He wanted to be near me but still allowed me the space to fall apart in peace. It was his way of letting me know I wasn't alone. I respected it, but I was too broken up to thank him.

Once I'd finally settled my cries, I uttered to him, "Come in," I told him through the curtain.

"You sure?"

I pulled back the curtain so that he could see me nod. "Yeah."

Cy kept his tired eyes trained on me as he stripped bare. He stepped inside, pulling me into his strong arms. His embrace was solid, grounding me like an anchor. I buried my face in his warm chest, tears soaking his tattoos.

He stroked the back of my head. "You're safe," he murmured, his voice steady. "You did what you had to do. He would have killed you both. As far as everything else, it's taken care of."

I nodded, unable to find my words. The adrenaline had faded, leaving me vulnerable and broken. But Cy held me up. His strength became my foundation. I felt the warmth of his love and the depth of his feelings for me without him uttering a single word. The water continued to pour down as we clung to each other. As the steam rose around us, I knew I wasn't alone. I had Cy, our son, and a future filled with the protection of Cy and The Spades.

"Thank you," I whispered, my voice hoarse. "For everything—for saving us."

He kissed my forehead, his fingers brushing away my tears. "Always."

I turned away, and we silently washed our bodies, scrubbing every inch of ourselves clean. I wasn't sure about him, but I knew I'd been trying to wash the ick of my sins away, praying they'd magically slide down the drain. Cy reached forward and turned off the shower before stepping out. He quickly dried himself off before wrapping the towel around his body.

"Dry off and meet me in the bedroom. Don't bother getting dressed."

My eyes widened briefly before relaxing back into their natural state. We hadn't spoken about our intimate moment since it happened and were about to run smack dab into another one. I tip-toed out of the bathroom to find Cy sitting on the edge of the bed, rubbing something between his palms with the sheets turned down.

"What is this?" I asked as a yawn slipped past my lips.

"Lay down on your stomach," he instructed.

I inched toward the bed, noticing the bottle of baby oil on the nightstand. "What is this about?"

"I want to make sure you sleep, Kendyl. You need to forget about everything and rest," he declared, prioritizing my comfort as if nothing else mattered.

My shoulders were constantly tense, and a massage would help alleviate my stress. I followed his instructions and lay naked on my stomach. Cy's hands were strong yet gentle as he worked out the knots in my muscles. He started with long, sweeping strokes, using the lavender-scented baby oil.

"Everything feel okay?" he asked, checking in on me.

My eyes eased shut. "It's perfect," I answered, feeling the tension dissipate.

His tough-skinned hands worked their way down my spine, finding the tight knots in my lower back. Next, he moved from my ass down to the back of my thighs and legs. Cy rubbed my calf muscles, easing the tightness from hours of sitting in the car before landing at my toes. They tingled as he massaged each foot, the scented oil relaxing my skin.

Somewhere along the line, his touch became instinctual, as if he were reading my body. My breath hitched when I felt his kisses against the back of my thigh. He kissed a trail, bouncing in a zig-zagged motion from one leg to the other before his tongue slid against the crack of my ass. Before I knew it, Cy had cracked open my legs and was sucking on my clit from behind like a newborn to his mother's nipple.

"Oooh shit," I squealed.

I squirmed at first, but soon, the command of his tongue gave way to pleasure. I breathed deeply, surrendering to his healing oral touch.

"Mmm, fuck. Keep going, don't stop," I purred, my mouth gaped open.

My eyes were clamped shut as I tooted my ass up in the air, allowing him to get better leverage underneath me. Cy slid underneath me like a mechanic underneath the hood of his favorite car and licked my pussy as I bucked my hips against his bearded face.

I moaned. "Yes, yes, yes! Oh my God, I'm cumming!"

As soon as I came, I drifted into a deep sleep, feeling lighter, as if all my worries had evaporated into thin air.

Chop

I slowly eased my arm from underneath Kendyl's sleeping body. After gently sitting up and swinging my legs over the edge of my bed, I paused. I cast my gaze over my shoulder, watching her. Kendyl's chest rose and fell rhythmically, her face serene in sleep. The soft strands of her dark, curly hair spilled across the pillow, and for a moment, I forgot the chaos that had brought us to where we were. We'd been through hell together—the kind of hell that left permanent scars on the soul. The kind that made a nigga question everything he believed in. But as I sat there, I felt a strange sense of peace wash over me. Maybe it was the way her breathing steadied or the knowledge that she was safe with me.

Just hours ago, the worst scenarios imaginable were playing through my head on a loop. I thought I was going to lose her and my son. I hated seeing Kendyl's eyes wide with terror, the blood stains on her clothes, and her hands trembling as she dealt with the aftermath. But I'd never say I wasn't glad that nigga or her neighbor were dead. They were a threat to Kendyl and Cree, and I wouldn't let anybody breathing harm them—not on my watch. As I watched her sleep, I thought about how much darkness her eyes had witnessed—the fear, the blood, the life draining out of a man she'd once cared for. But somehow, she'd found solace in the comfort of my bed. I was grateful for that.

Unable to stay still, I padded toward the door. The carpeted steps creaked beneath my bare feet as I headed downstairs. I needed answers and reassurance. I pulled out my phone and dialed Nitro's number.

"Yo," I said when the call connected. "Anybody report any movement from Demon's crew?"

Nitro's voice crackled through the line. "Not yet."

"What about the cops?"

"Not a peep. We cleaned the place good."

"And they packed up all the rest of her and Cree's things?"

"Yeah. It's en route to you now."

I exhaled, relief flooding through me as I sat on the couch with my phone pressed to my ear. "Good. She's been through enough. She's staying here from now on."

"Got it," Nitro said. "And Chop?"

"Yeah?"

"Take care of her, nigga. We got y'all."

I hung up, staring out the window. The Spades were my family; they'd protect Kendyl and my son as fiercely as they protected their own. I'd keep her safe, even if it meant facing whoever lurked beyond the shadows. My attention wavered toward the stairs, snapping me out of my thoughts. I glanced at where the wooden banister curved gracefully. And then I heard a faint, sleepy voice calling out from above.

"Mommy?"

My heart skipped a beat. I tossed the phone on the couch and bounded up the stairs. At the top stood Cree, his tousled curls sticking up in all directions. His eyes were wide, and his little hand clutched his stuffed bear.

"I had a bad dream," Cree whispered, his voice trembling.

I scooped him up, cradling him against my chest. "It's okay, lil man," I murmured. "You're safe now. What was the dream about?"

Cree buried his face in my shoulder. "Monsters," he said. "They were under my bed, and Mommy wasn't there."

His small voice made my heart clench. "Mommy's sleeping," I said, carrying him downstairs to the living room. I settled onto the couch, and Cree curled against me. "We need to let her rest."

"But I miss her," Cree whispered.

I smoothed his hair. "I know you do. But you have me now. And I promise I'll be here for you."

Cree looked up, his eyes searching my face for answers. "Are you my daddy?"

I hesitated, then nodded. "Yes, Cree. I'm your dad."

His face lit up. "I always wanted a dad," he said. "Can we do stuff together?"

My throat tightened. "Absolutely," I said. "We'll build forts, play catch, and—"

"And ride a bike!" Cree interrupted, his excitement contagious.

I chuckled. "A bike, huh? Well, guess what? I'm going to get you the coolest bike ever. I'ma see if I can find you a ride-on motorcycle so you can ride like daddy."

Cree's eyes widened. "Really?"

"Really," I confirmed. "And we'll ride it together, wind in our hair and everything."

Cree snuggled closer. "That's a good idea," he said. "You're my hero, Daddy."

My chest swelled. "And you're mine," I whispered.

I knew we had a lot to learn about each other, but I was ready—ready to be present and to be the dad Cree deserved. Before tucking him back into bed, I gave him a super-secret snack—an Oreo cookie from the kitchen, while I put in an overnight delivery order online for his ride-on motorcycle.

I kissed my son's forehead and whispered, "Get some rest so you'll be ready for our motorcycle adventure."

MY LIVING ROOM WAS A JUMBLE OF CARDBOARD BOXES AND memories the following day. My men had retrieved the rest of Kendyl's belongings from her old place, and she was sorting through the remnants of her past. She sat cross-legged on the floor near the couch, surrounded by open boxes. Old photo albums spilled their contents—rare, faded pictures of her childhood, us, and other moments she'd rather forget. I watched her from the kitchen for a few minutes before walking over.

"Hey," I said softly, crouching beside her. "How's it going?"

Kendyl looked up, her expression a mix of nostalgia and determination. "It's... strange," she admitted. "Seeing all this shit again."

I nodded. "Take your time. I'll keep Cree entertained."

I scooped up our son, who was busy stacking Kendyl's old shoes into a makeshift tower. Cree's laughter echoed through the room, and I smiled. "How about you and I take your new motorcycle to the park?" I asked him, and he clapped his little hands in agreement.

Kendyl smiled. "You two be safe and have fun."

"We will," I assured her.

The air outside smelled of freshly cut grass, and the sun's warmth wrapped around us like a cozy blanket. As I strolled to the nearby playground, I watched Cree ride a few paces ahead of me on his electric three-wheeler motorcycle. He squealed as the wind ruffled his coils. I pulled out my phone to take my first picture of him before making it my new wallpaper. I wanted to always be able to see what black boy joy looked like.

Cree's innocent laughter echoed through the sun-drenched park as I chased him to the jungle gym. His tiny sneakers kicked up mulch as we circled the playground. I pushed him on the swing while watching other parents—mothers and fathers—interacting with their kids. It felt like I'd stepped into a parallel universe—one where I was a different man with a different story. But I wouldn't change it for the world.

My phone buzzed as I was about to push him higher to watch him soar. My sister Nina's name appeared on the screen, and I quickly tapped accept. When the call connected, I saw her face framed by her faux locs and oversized glasses.

"Wassup, Nina!" I said, wiping sweat from my brow.

Nina's eyes widened as she took in the scene behind me. "Hey, big head. What are you doing?"

"I'm at the park."

"The park? Since when have you been going to the park?"

"Since this," I said before flipping the camera around to show her Cree swinging.

"Cyrus Demetri Bailey, who's that cutie pie?"

I grinned. "Meet Cree, your nephew. Surprise!"

Nina's jaw dropped. "You had a whole fucking child and didn't tell me!"

"Trust me, it's all still new," I explained. "I just found out I had a son."

"With..." she probed, brows heightened.

"Kendyl."

At the drop of her name, Nina's questions tumbled out like leaves caught in a gust of wind. "How? When? Why did she—? Why didn't you—"

I interrupted her. "You still tryna come out for that visit? The doors open for you to meet Cree and ask his mother yourself."

Nina scoffed. "Don't tempt me," she said, her voice trembling. "I'll book a flight right now!"

I chuckled. "You're welcome to. And trust me, Kendyl would be happy as hell to see you."

Nina's eyes sparkled with happy tears. "Okay, okay! Chicago, here I come! Now turn the camera around and let me see my handsome nephew again! Hey Stink! Auntie Nina can't wait to meet you!"

Forty-five minutes later, we returned. The apartment had transformed in a minor but noticeable way. Kendyl had hung a string of fairy lights across the living room window, casting a warm glow. A potted plant sat on the windowsill, its leaves reaching for the sunlight. And in her hands was a worn leather journal—the same one she'd taken when she left our shared apartment all those years ago. I remembered the late nights when Kendyl would write, her erratic, mismatched thoughts freely spilling onto the pages. We were young, in love, and full of dreams. But life had a way of tearing shit apart.

She opened the journal, her fingers tracing the taped-in Polaroid of our headboard with the engraved initials—C & K. "Remember doing this?" she asked.

I nodded, my throat tight. "One of our wild, drunken nights," I answered, knowing the pages of her journal were filled with our past road trips on my bike and the secrets we shared.

She flipped to a page, her voice soft. "This entry," she said. "The night we sat underneath the stars after sneaking into that concert. You got my lips tatted on your neck and promised me forever."

I remembered everything—the imprint of her red lipstick on the napkin, Kendyl's laughter, the sweet taste of her lips after the burn of the tattoo needle. "I meant all that shit too," I whispered.

Her eyes met mine. "I know. But forever isn't always what we think."

Before I could respond, Cree barreled into the living room, his tiny socks sliding on the hardwood floor. His face lit up when he saw us. He raced over, inserting his slim body between his mother and me. He inserted himself between us as Kendyl and I sat on opposite ends of the couch, putting a pin in our conversation.

"Mommy! Daddy!" Cree panted, his cheeks flushed. "I'm hungry!"

Kendyl knelt, brushing a lock of hair from his forehead. "Hey, buddy. Hungry, huh? What do you want for dinner?"

Cree's eyes widened with excitement. "Pizza!"

Kendyl held up a finger. "Okay. Let's ask daddy if we can order pizza tonight."

Cree turned to me, his expression serious. "Daddy, can we have pizza?"

I chuckled as I ruffled his coils. "Pizza it is, champ. Let's order it together. What kind do you want? Pepperoni? Sausage? Pineapple?"

His small features twisted in disgust. "Pineapple? Ew! Yucky! I want pepperoni!"

"You got it."

And just like that, our conversation about second chances and forever was momentarily forgotten. As I dialed the nearest pizza place, Cree danced around the room, chanting, *"Pizza party! Pizza party!"*

"You're spoiling him rotten, you know that?" Kendyl stated it as more of a fact than a question.

"So what?"

She smirked while playfully rolling her eyes. "Whatever. We may be having a pizza party, but you're still eating your vegetables! Pick a green, Cree! Broccoli or salad?"

"Ew, yucky broccoli! I don't like broccoli, Mommy!"

"So, then salad?"

"Salad! Salad!" he agreed before returning to his original chant.

A half-hour later, the living room was filled with the aroma of freshly baked pizza. Kendyl stood at the table, arranging paper plates and napkins, while Cree clapped his hands excitedly.

"Mommy, pizza!" Cree giggled, his eyes wide with anticipation.

Kendyl grinned, her eyes sparkling. "Yes, baby boy! It's pizza *and* salad time!"

After dinner, I scooped Cree into my arms, promising him a bubble bath adventure and that we'd build a pillow fort after. Kendyl headed to the kitchen to clean up.

Sudsy giggles echoed from the bathroom as I playfully washed him up, scrubbing away the day's dirt. There was something to note about the ordinary moments—the mess, the laughter, the warmth of our close-knit family. Whenever I looked at Cree or Kendyl, I felt a rush of love flow into my heart. It was something I'd ever felt before. I finally knew what it meant to have unconditional love for someone. Kendyl was my soulmate, bringing me peace when life got too chaotic.

Once Cree was dressed for bed, the three of us settled onto the couch. The soft glow of string lights she'd draped across the window created the dopest vibe. The coffee table was adorned with a bowl of popcorn, and Kendyl sat cross-legged on the opposite side of the couch. She wore a loose-fitting sweater and leggings while watching me scratch my head.

"What?" I probed, catching her gaze.

"I could retwist them for you. All you have to do is ask."

My brow lurched toward my hairline. "Word?"

"Yeah."

"Say less."

I got up to grab my loc gel and coconut oil before sitting on the floor between her legs. The animated movie's opening credits rolled. I kept my eyes fixed on the TV screen as my locs spilled over her thighs. Kendyl's fingers moved skillfully through my hair, separating each section as she retwisted each strand carefully. We fell into a comfortable silence, the room filling with the scent of buttered popcorn and greased scalp. Kendyl's touch was delicate and focused, her talent evident in every twist reaching past my shoulders. I closed my eyes, savoring the moment.

As the movie climaxed, Kendyl finished the last loc and leaned back to admire her work. We settled back into the couch, and she rested her head against my shoulder. I stole glances at her when I could, her profile illuminated by the screen. The soft glow high-lighted the bridge of her nose and the curve of her lips. She was beauty personified. My heart raced. I'd never felt so content, so sure.

The words bubbled up inside me, threatening to spill out. *Marry me.* But every time I parted my lips to speak, I hesitated. We'd been through so much. *Is it too soon? Too risky?* As the movie soundtrack played softly, I decided to wait. Not because I doubted my feelings but because I respected her vulnerability. I'd propose someday when it felt right. But in the meantime, I'd hold onto her, knowing that I was content with our imperfect, joy-filled moments.

Kendyl

*T**hree days later.*

The morning sunlight peeked through the curtains, casting a warm glow on the wooden floor. I rubbed my eyes, disoriented for a moment. Then I remembered I was in Cy's house, the place that had become my refuge. I descended the stairs, and there they were: Cy and Cree, shirtless and perched on the couch. Cy clad in basketball shorts, and Cree in his superhero training underwear. Each was holding a bowl of sugary Froot Loops. The TV blared some wacky, colorful cartoons, and Cree's laughter filled the room. My heart swelled. I'd never imagined this—a family scene so simple yet overwhelming. Cy glanced up, catching my gaze. His eyes crinkled at the corners, and he waved me over next to them.

"Morning. Join us," he said, his voice soft.

I hesitated, torn between joy and uncertainty. I'd fled an abusive relationship, and Cy had been my unexpected savior. But there we were—two adults with a child who hadn't discussed the future beyond survival. It was like every time we started to tip-toe around the discussion, something always got in the way—sex, an unexpected kidnapping, and *more* sex. I shuffled into the kitchen, the floor cool beneath my feet. Pouring cereal into a bowl, I wondered how to raise the unspoken questions. Cy shared his bed with me, welcomed Cree and me into his home, and encouraged me to make it my own. We'd agreed to take it slow and had done anything but. We were in a gray area. Realistically, I didn't know what came next.

I returned to the living room, sitting cross-legged on the right side of the couch. Cree squirmed between us, his spoon dipping into his bowl for more Froot Loops. Cy's gaze lingered on me, and I knew he was wrestling with his own thoughts. I studied him—the lines etched on his face, the kindness in his eyes. He'd rescued us, yes, but it was more than that. He'd given us a chance at a fresh start.

"I'm thinking about getting a job," I blurted out. "I don't want to be a burden."

"You're not a burden. Cree loves being here. And I..." He hesitated, then took a deep breath. "I just don't want you to feel like you gotta make a move right now."

My spoon clinked against the bowl. "I'm used to being independent, Cy. I don't want to rely on anyone. Not even you," I admitted as I stirred my cereal, avoiding his eyes.

"I told you I want you here," he said, his voice steady. "You and Cree. Not just because of what happened, but I don't want you to feel trapped or dependent."

My eyes welled up, and I immediately felt overwhelmed. "I don't know how to do this..."

He reached for my hand. "We'll figure it out. Taking things slow, remember?"

I scoffed while stirring my cereal. "Right."

He cleared his throat. "Listen, the club is running a booth at our annual community carnival tonight. I told everybody I'd staff it for a couple of hours. You and Cree wanna roll too?"

Cree's face lit up before I had the chance to respond. "Mommy, I wanna go to the fun place! Can we go to the fun place?"

A slow smile spread across my face. "Yeah, baby boy. We can go."

<hr>

THE CARNIVAL WHIRRED WITH LIFE—THE AIR SWEET WITH THE scent of sticky cotton candy and the distant hum of rides. Colorful tents lined the makeshift path, their canopy flags flapping in the breeze. I watched as Cree's eyes widened, his little hand tugging at mine.

"Mommy, look!" he exclaimed, pointing at the Ferris wheel. Its giant neon-blinking rods spun against the sky, each cart carrying laughter and excitement.

Cy grinned, ruffling Cree's hair. "You wanna ride that, lil man?"

Cree nodded vigorously, and my heart melted. It was our first outing as a family. "We'll ride some rides a little later, okay?" I promised.

We arrived at The Spades Motorcycle Club booth right in the heart of it all. It stood proudly amidst the colorful tents, cotton candy stalls, and the slow whirl of the Ferris wheel. The booth was a large black tent adorned with their club's banners and fairy lights. A sign across the front proclaimed: "The Spades MC: Ride or Die!"

Inside the booth was a riot of good company. Bikers in their leather club vests chatted with locals. One biker with his sleeves rolled up to reveal his inked arms handled the tattoo chair. For a small donation, anyone could get a temporary Spades MC tattoo. Kids lined up, wide-eyed, as he applied the washable designs. There was a customized Harley-Davidson right out front to draw in visitors. Its polished chrome gleamed under the twinkling fairy lights. The owner reeled in locals with entertaining stories of cross-country rides, breakdowns during natural disasters, and the general thrill of the open road.

Cree and I guarded the charity jar—a glass container filled with bills and coins. The Spades donated all the proceeds to the local children's hospital. I winked and waved at onlookers, urging them to contribute. "Change for children," I said, my voice gentle. "Help us heal hearts!" Some dropped in spare change; others emptied their wallets. Regardless, my smile never wavered.

There was a black leather jacket hanging on display. It bore The Spade's emblem—a hissing viper coiled around a black spade. Cy explained that they raffled one off every year. The winner got to wear it with pride, knowing they supported local community causes. I bought a ticket in support, inspired by it all. As the carnival lights glimmered and laughter echoed, I learned The Spades weren't the ruthless biker gang I'd made them out to be in my mind. They were a family woven into the fabric of Chicago—a strong brotherhood that rode together, had each other's backs, and gave back to their community.

After spending a couple of hours working the booth, the three of us wandered through the carnival. The sun started to set, but a lively mix of activities was happening. Cree dragged us toward the carousel, the bumper cars, and then the dizzying tilt-a-whirl. We played endless games. Cy aimed for the tricky bottlenecks, hoping to win a giant stuffed animal. Laughter erupted from us all as his rings missed and landed on their targets. In the end, Cy won him a stuffed monkey, and as he proudly handed it to him, a new memory tugged at my heart.

The giant Ferris wheel spun gracefully, pausing when our cart reached the top. The view from above offered breathtaking sights of the city and surrounding areas. Cy held my hand, stroking it gently as the cart slowly rocked with the breeze. After our ride, we wandered over to the row of food trucks offering everything from juicy burgers to funnel cakes. The aroma of fried treats and the buttery scent of freshly popped popcorn wafted through the air. Cree clutched a blue cloud of sweet cotton candy, his face sticky with delight as we approached a talented artist's face-painting station. I watched her transform children into butterflies, fairies, superheroes, and jungle animals. Cy and I snapped photos as Cree proudly displayed his Spiderman-painted face.

As the night's end approached, our anticipation built for the grand finale: the fireworks show. The three of us gathered on the grassy hill, keeping our eyes fixed on the night sky. The first explosion sent shimmering sparkles shooting upward before painting the darkness with vibrant colors—ruby reds, emerald greens, and golden yellows. The crowd "*oohed*" and "*ahhed*" around us as each burst lit up the night. Cy pulled me close, nuzzling his face into the side of my neck. I twisted my neck, and our lips met. It was just the two of us and the starbursts above for that brief moment. Gratitude and longing mingled on my lips.

He whispered a gentle reminder in my ear. "You're safe now. I won't let anyone hurt you."

I believed him, even though I still felt so brittle and broken. Being around the motorcycle club—Cy's family—had sheltered me and unknowingly helped nurse me back to life.

As we drove home, Cree's heavy eyelids drooped. The carnival lights faded in the rearview mirror, replaced by the quiet darkness of suburban streets. I glanced at Cy, his knuckles gripping the steering wheel. I traced the edge of the stuffed bear's ear as Cy slowed the car to a stop at a red light.

He cleared his throat. "You have fun today?"

"It was great. Cree had a blast. You see him knocked out back there with his mouth wide open." I chuckled. "Thank you for inviting us."

He laughed alongside me. "Yeah, lil man is slumped. And you're welcome. I thought it might be good for you to see the club in a different light."

"It was good. Regardless of how I feel about your motorcycle club, I appreciate what they did for Cree and me—what y'all did."

He hesitated, then spoke softly. "We saved you, and you saved me, too." I leaned my head against the window as the light turned green. Cy eased the car forward. "So, you really thinking about getting a job?" he quizzed, his voice slicing through the silence.

I turned to him, my pulse quickening. "Yeah. Like I said earlier, I don't want to depend on anyone."

"You won't be," he said. "And Cree needs stability."

"But—"

Cy sucked his teeth before reaching for my hand. "*Fuck it.* I love you, Kendyl. I've loved you since the first time I met you when you looked at me and stole my breath right out of my chest. I don't wanna be without you or our family."

I swallowed the melon-sized lump in my throat. "And the club?"

He sighed. "It's part of who I am. I'm the president, and I know that life ain't easy. But I want you with me, Kendyl. Not because of the club, but because you're where I wanna be. The club is my family, but you and Cree are my home. I've been fighting the urge to ask you to marry a nigga because I know you've been through hell and back, but I'm standing ten toes down behind you, Kendyl, until my last breath."

My breath hitched. "Cy..."

"You don't have to give me an answer now. I just wanted you to know where I'm at with this shit. I'm moving on your time. Whenever you're ready, I'll be here," he assured me.

I scoffed while slowly shaking my head. "You think it's that easy, huh?"

"What?"

"Picking up where we left off, falling in love, and living happily ever after."

He shrugged. "I never said it would be, but I'm willing to find out."

"Mmm."

He glanced at me before darting his attention back to the road. "Whatever you're over there fighting internally right now, I think it's an excuse."

My brows hitched. "Excuse me?"

"You heard me. Another excuse for you to run."

"I don't run."

He rolled his eyes. "That's bullshit, Kendyl. You're *always* running, and you know it. You ran from me, then—"

I cut him a stern glare. "Don't you dare say it."

"I wasn't. What I was going to say was your ass is afraid of commitment."

"Just because I want to be independent, I'm afraid to commit?" I snapped, making sure my words bit without raising my voice. I wagged my head. "You don't understand."

"Cut the shit, Kendyl. It's me. I'm the one you left. And you did it because you got scared. You feel these big-ass feelings, and then you get scared of what they mean and how gushy they make you feel when you try so hard to be tough. And until you admit that shit, it doesn't matter how many times I tell you you're safe or how many ways I show you how much I love you, it'll never be enough for you," he spat as he wheeled the car into the driveway.

He killed the engine and exited the car without waiting for my rebuttal. His silence and cold shoulder let me know our heated discussion had turned our fun-filled family outing sour. My thoughts ran wildly, bouncing around and jumbling to the front of my mind. *He's wrong, right? Well... he's not one hundred percent wrong—more like ninety. Okay, okay, like seventy-five. Shit. I've been known to be a little flighty, but it's for good reason, right? When you know, you know. Unless you don't. Fuck.*

———

AFTER STRIPPING OFF CREE'S CARNIVAL CLOTHES AND TUCKING him into bed, I gave Cy his space by showering in the hall bathroom. Twenty minutes later, I tip-toed down the hall to see Cy's bedroom door slightly ajar. I wasn't sure if I wanted to pick up where we left off, apologize, or go to bed mad. By the time I reached the door, I already had the words ready to fall off my lips.

"I'm sorry," I spoke up from the doorway, eyeing him as he sat on the edge of the bed with his locs tied up in a high bun and a fresh pair of basketball shorts on.

He shot me a stern glare that softened as the seconds passed. "I don't wanna argue."

I shook my head. "Me either," I said as I stepped inside and eased the door shut behind me. "I left... I left because I knew it was only a matter of time before you left me."

He grunted. "You didn't know shit then, and you sure as hell don't know shit now. I was ten toes down for you when we were together. You were just too scared and too insecure to see it."

"I can admit I made a panicked decision back then. You know my past, Cy. Sometimes I can be... *fickle*," I acknowledged, my chest deflating with a hard sigh as I tightened my towel around my body.

"Like I said, you're a runner. You can't tell me shit I don't already know about you, girl. I know you like the back of my hand. Just like I know you still love me, even if you're too scared to say it out loud."

My breath hitched, and my palms moistened at his revelation. "Cy—"

He raised his hand, putting a pause in my sentence. "I don't wanna hear you say it now. I want you to want to tell me you love me, Kendyl. I want you to want it so bad the fuckin' words are literally burning your tongue. That's what it was like for me—what it's *still* like for me."

"Cy—"

"Let me finish," he interjected again. "All I want to hear you say for the rest of the night is my name."

My brows heightened toward my swooped edges. Before I could arrange my next string of words, Cy stepped forward and pressed his lips against mine. We kissed as if our lips craved the opportunity to piece together our broken narrative. He picked me up and carried me to the bed before laying me down. We kissed slowly, savoring our passionate make-out session. I may not have had all the answers, but I did have the moment, and I planned to show him how much I cared about him through my actions.

I flipped him onto his back and straddled him before kissing down his chest. My lips peppered soft kisses down his washboard abs down to the elastic lining of his basketball shorts. He relaxed his posture before inching his shorts and boxers down to his ankles. I dropped to my knees and took his semi-hard dick into my warm mouth. My hand slid up and down his shaft as I sucked on the head. I licked the tip before spitting on it and running my thick tongue up and down his long shaft.

He growled as I eased his length in and out my mouth. "Mmm, yeah. I like that nasty shit. Spit on it again," he demanded.

I put my lips into an O-shape before deep-throating him. I flashed my seductive eyes up at him as I came up for air with spit dribbling off my bottom lip. He pushed my wet ringlets out of my face as he came to a standing position, fully stepping out of his boxers. Cy rested both hands on his lower back, thrusting his stiff rod forward as I sucked and jacked off the tip.

He grunted with pleasure. "Oooh shit."

Cy palmed the back of my head, thrusting the tip of his thick dick in and out of my mouth. I opened my mouth wide, brushing and flicking my tongue over the head. Before nearing his climax, Cy pulled me back onto the bed, and I laid on my back. He mounted me, the silver locket dangling in my face as his girth spread me open. He leaned in close, pressing his forehead against mine. He stared deep into my eyes, refusing to break eye contact before he kissed me.

He gripped my waist, picking up the pace as he had one hand wrapped around my neck and the other pressed into my stomach, stroking deep. Before I knew it, Cy had both my legs pinned above my head as he gripped my neck and fucked me senseless.

I moaned. "Oooh, fuck. It's soooo deep, Cy," I purred as he plowed in and out of me.

Cy pinned my ankles together, holding my legs over his left shoulder while he dug me out, taking out his unspoken frustrations with each stroke. He flipped me over onto my stomach before his lips devoured my pussy from behind. I fell victim to the soft lashes of his tongue against my clit.

"Oooh, shit," I hissed, sucking in air through my teeth as I reached around to grab his locs.

He licked up and down my slit, switching between thrashing my folds while he finger fucked me from behind and sucking my clit. His lips teased me, edging me toward my climax before he pulled away. I drew in a sharp breath as Cy pressed his strong hands into my spine, burying every inch of him deep inside me. Cy hunched forward into a C-curl, humping me like a jackrabbit and hitting my G-spot with each stroke.

"Does it feel good?" he probed as he smacked my ass.

"It feels so good! I fuckin' love it," I purred.

"What's my name?"

"Cy!"

"Is this still my pussy?"

I moaned, looking over my shoulder at him. "Yes, baby. It's yours. It's all yours!"

He pressed his chest against my back, bearing all his weight onto me as he stroked deep. "Say this, Cyrus Bailey's fuckin pussy," he demanded.

"Yes! It's Cyrus Bailey's fuckin' pussy, baby. You feel so fuckin' good," I cried, whimpering in pleasure.

The sheets crumpled in my grasp. All I heard was the smacking of my ass against his thighs and my repetitive moans until we switched into the reverse cowgirl position. Cy reached around to massage my clit as I eased up and down on him. My roaming hands caressed my breasts and tugged at my chocolate nipples. I leaned back, pressing my arm into his chest as my slippery wet pussy slid up and down his rod. Cy lifted me underneath my thighs, thrusting into me from underneath.

"Oooh fuck! Yes! Keep going! Shit, it's so deep!" I squealed while panting heavily. He strummed my clit, getting me wetter and wetter until I squirted. "Ooooh fuck! I'm cummminnggggg!" I screamed.

He gripped my waist and eased me forward, tooting my ass up in the air just before he penetrated me from the back again. I looked back at him while I threw it back, my warmth swallowing his dick whole.

"Mmm, shit, Cy. You fuck me so good, baby."

"Mmm, fuck yes," he growled, gently yanking my hair as he spilled his cum inside me.

We both crashed against the bed, faces pressed into the sheets. Breaking up to make-up never felt so good.

———

I woke up the following day to see Cy sitting on the edge of the bed, a mischievous grin on his lips.

"Guess what?" he whispered. "I have a surprise for you."

I blinked, still half-asleep. "What is it?"

He leaned closer. "Hurry up and get dressed. We're picking up my sister Nina from the airport in an hour. She's coming to visit."

Despite our age difference, Nina and I used to be somewhat close. I looked at her like the little sister I never had. My eyes widened. "Nina? I haven't seen her in years!"

Cy nodded. "She's excited, too. And Cree—well, he's about to meet his auntie."

The three of us arrived at the airport an hour later. I fidgeted near the arrivals gate. After a few minutes, the crowd shifted, and there she was—Nina, with her faux locs, oversized glasses, and a backpack slung over one shoulder. I stood holding Cree, watching as she and Cy rushed into each other's arms, squealing and laughing simultaneously.

"Nina!" I exclaimed. "You're here!"

Nina walked over and squeezed me tightly. "Kendyl! Damn girl, it's been forever! I missed you."

"I've missed you too," I told her before looking down at Cree as he stared up at Nina, wide-eyed and curious. "Cree, say hi to your auntie Nina."

One look at Cree, and her eyes sparkled with tears. She knelt, her smile warm and inviting. "Hey, cutie pie. I'm Auntie Nina." She scooped him up, cradling him in her arms, and whispered, "You're even more precious than I imagined."

I watched her heart swell with love as she looked at her nephew— the tiny fingers, the button nose, and his innocent eyes that held a universe of wonder. "I promise you I will be the best auntie you could ever have!"

Back home, Cree continued to study Nina, then held out his favorite toy truck. "Wanna play trucks?"

Nina laughed. "Yes! Of course, buddy."

Cy watched them interact for a little while without interruption, with pride in his eyes. "I'll keep Cree entertained. You girls go out and catch up," he encouraged.

I hesitated. "Are you sure?"

He kissed my forehead. "Absolutely. Enjoy your one-on-one time."

Nina gripped my hand and tugged me toward the door. "You heard the man. C'mon, girl. Let's get out of here before he changes his mind!"

THE RESTAURANT HUMMED WITH LIFE, THE CLATTER OF DISHES and snippets of conversation weaving around Nina and me. We sat in a cozy corner booth with our hands wrapped around piping hot coffee mugs.

"So, how's Maryland been treating you?" I inquired, stirring my latte. "How's college?"

Nina's eyes sparkled. "It's amazing! I'm majoring in marine biology. You know how much I love the ocean."

I chuckled. "You always did like being in the damn water."

But then Nina's expression shifted, her gaze piercing. "Kendyl, why did you leave my brother? And why didn't you tell him about that gorgeous little boy you two made together?"

My chest tightened. I knew there was only so long she'd let me go without bringing up the elephant in the room. I cleared my throat. "Listen, I didn't know I was pregnant when I left. But when I found out, I was scared out of my fucking mind, Nina. Scared of his ties to The Spades, scared of being abandoned again like how my parents left me. At the time, I thought I was protecting the baby from a life of... I don't know. It all sounds so pointless now."

"But you never called," Nina said softly. "He searched for you, Kendyl. You broke him. I'd never seen him so lost after you left."

My throat ached. "I thought it was better this way. I didn't want to burden him. I didn't want him to choose between us or the club, so I chose for him. It was selfish. I know that now," I admitted with a sigh.

Nina leaned closer. "He's your family too. You're not a burden."

"I don't want to lose my independence or myself in him again, Nina. And the more I stick around, the more I feel myself slipping."

"How have things been with my brother since you moved back?" Nina questioned, her eyes knowing.

I traced the rim of my mug. "Complicated... yet painfully simple."

Nina raised an eyebrow. "Have you been arguing?"

I wagged my head. "No. It's the opposite, really. Sometimes, it's almost like I never left, like the years somehow melted away. And then other times, I wake up in the middle of the night not knowing where I am, afraid I'm going to wake up one day and not know his skin from mine. You know how crazy in love we were once upon a time, Nina. I mean, I know you were a little younger, but I can't handle being last on your brother's list of priorities again. I won't survive, and I've got a son to raise this time around."

"A son that's half his, Kendyl. Remember?"

A huff of air burst past my nose. "I mean, what the fuck, Nina? The main reason I left him in the first place was because he always put me second to that fucking club, and now I come back four years later, and he's the president! What's really changed besides the fact that we have a kid together?"

"You don't think he loves you?"

"I know he does. He even said he wanted to marry me."

"And how do you feel about that?"

"I'm not sure," I admitted. "I wanna trust it, but I still have my reservations. What do you think about all this?"

Nina grinned. "I think love is messy. But it's always worth it, especially when it's real. You deserve happiness. And so does he. Why not have it with each other?"

Just thinking about officially starting over with Cy had me shitting bricks. As we left the restaurant, Nina glanced at me before handing me her phone. "Call him."

I hesitated. "And say what?"

"That you two need some one-on-one time out of the house to talk, breathe, and let loose. Do whatever you two got to do to make this shit official again," she encouraged.

I sighed. "What about Cree?"

Nina snatched the phone from me and called her brother on FaceTime. He picked up on the third ring. "Hello?"

"Listen, big brother. You're taking your beautiful ass baby mama on a hot date tonight, and I'm watching Cree! I aim to teach him as many trending TikTok dances as possible while you're gone, so don't rush back, okay?"

I blinked. "Nina, I—"

"Nope," Nina interrupted. "No excuses! You good with that, Cy?"

"Yeah. I'm good."

"Great. It's settled. Now we're off to the mall to find her something sexy to wear! Okay, byeeeeeee!" Nina rambled before quickly ending the call.

THE TRENDY BOUTIQUE INSIDE THE MALL WAS BATHED IN A soft, flattering light. Racks of dresses in various colors and styles surrounded us as we sorted through them. The air smelled faintly of perfume, and the hum of other shoppers lost in their own fashion crises created a gentle buzz.

Nina held up a crimson option from a nearby rack. "What about this one? It's giving confidence, *and* it's your size."

I fingered the silk fabric. "I don't know if I can—"

Nina's eyes softened. "You can. And you will. Now go try it on!"

Minutes later, I twirled in front of the mirror, the red dress hugging my curves in all the right places.

Nina grinned from ear to ear. "Girrrllll, that's the one! You look stunning! That color is perfect for you. I told you it was giving confidence! Tens all around the board!"

"You really think so? It's been ages since I dressed up for anyone other than my son."

"Girl, you're not just dressing up for anyone. You're dressing up for destiny. Four years, Kendyl! Four years since you've been out with my brother. Tonight's your chance to get that old thang back."

My fingers traced the delicate fabric on the dress. "Ugh. But what if it's awkward?"

"It won't be! Now, do me a favor and tell your anxiety she's a lying ass ho and to shut the fuck up forever! You've both grown. Plus, you're not just '*Kendyl, the mom*' anymore. You're Kendyl, the grown-ass woman ready to rewrite her love story with her soulmate."

I gazed at myself in the mirror while taking a deep breath. "Okay, fine. I'll get the dress."

"Hell yeah, you will!" Nina cheered. "Cyrus Bailey ain't gonna know what hit him."

Chop

I stood at the foot of the stairs, my heart stumbling out frantic beats. The soft glow of the light illuminated Kendyl's silhouette as she descended. She wore a crimson dress that clung to her curves, accentuating every graceful line. Red was my favorite color, and she looked damn good in it. My breath caught in my throat as I licked my lips. She looked good enough to eat.

"Beautiful," I whispered, unable to tear my eyes away. She blushed, her cherry-painted lips matching the hue of her dress. I leaned in, brushing my lips against her cheek, savoring the warmth of her skin. "You tryna make me go brick in front of everybody?"

She tilted her head, her eyes searching mine as she smirked. "Maybe."

Cree was perched on the bottom step, watching us with wide-eyed curiosity. "What do you think, Cree? Doesn't Mommy look pretty?" I asked him.

He nodded. "I like your dress, Mommy."

Nina waved us toward the door. "You kids have fun now. Be good to her, Bighead!"

As we left, Cree waved from the living room window, his stuffed monkey clutched tightly. In the car, the engine's hum filled the silence. Kendyl fidgeted with the hem of her dress, her voice barely audible.

"I was nervous about tonight," she admitted.

"Why?"

"I don't know. I guess it feels real, you know?"

I glanced at her, understanding flooding my chest. "Yeah. It does."

We drove through the familiar streets, memories intertwining with the present. She turned to me with a hopeful look in her eyes. "So, where exactly are we going? I know Nina threw this on the both of us at the last minute."

I grinned, keeping the surprise to myself. "You'll see," I teased. "But I promise, it'll be worth the wait."

Truthfully, I only had a couple of hours to put together a suitable date for some one-on-one time with Kendyl. I knew she'd always had an appreciation for fine dining. Plus, we both loved Italian food. So, I set up dinner reservations at an Italian restaurant and then planned to take her to the clubhouse afterward to unwind and bond some more before going home.

We stepped inside the cozy Italian restaurant called La Dolce Vita. Its dimly lit ambiance, rustic wooden tables, and the aroma of garlic and basil created the perfect vibe for our special night. The female hostess led us up a curving staircase to the rooftop terrace, where the soft sounds of a jazz trio filled the air. Their melodic tunes and the twinkling fairy lights overhead added an extra layer of charm to the candlelit scene. I'd reserved a private corner table adorned with flickering candles and a single red rose. A string of sparkling lights adorned the railings, casting a soft glow over the table. Surrounding us was the city's skyline stretching out for miles and miles.

Kendyl's eyes widened as I pulled out her chair. "Wow. This is absolutely beautiful!"

"I'm glad you like it."

"Like it? I love it. Look at the view! It's breathtaking."

"Nothing is as breathtaking as you," I affirmed, eyes trained on her.

The waiter approached our table, clad in crisp black and white attire. "Good evening. Welcome to La Dolce Vita. May I take your drink orders?"

I glanced at Kendyl. "We'll have the chef's special. And a bottle of your best white wine."

Kendyl agreed with a nod. "Sounds perfect."

Between courses, she shared intimate stories of her birth story with Cree, how it was just the two of them when she took him to the beach for his first birthday, and other silly memories of his childhood that I hadn't been around for. Her words made me think of all the other important things I'd missed—the sleepless nights, countless diaper changes, his first steps and words. As unhappy as I was about it, all the sacrifices she'd made to ensure he was raised right only deepened my gratitude. The missed career opportunities, the nights spent comforting him when he was sick, the rare, uninterrupted moments of silence stolen for herself—she'd given so much. Undoubtedly, she'd done a hell of a job raising him. I couldn't have hand-picked a better mother for my son than Kendyl. She was one of one. As I sat there, I vowed to keep telling her how much she meant to me, how her love had shaped our son for the better, and how I never planned to let her go.

Kendyl's innocent giggles echoed through the narrow streets as we left the restaurant, fueled by the chilled bottle of Sauvignon Blanc we'd shared. After a thirty-minute ride to the city's outskirts, The Spades clubhouse loomed ahead—a fortress of leather, steel, and solidarity. I led her through the heavy door, where the bass-heavy music vibrated the floor. The familiar scent of motor oil and freedom enveloped us like a warm hug. An instant smile spread across my face.

"Follow me," I said, slipping my hand in hers.

Upstairs, I unlocked the door to my office. She stepped inside, her heels click-clacking against the hardwood floor. The room was neat, the walls adorned with framed photos of past rides and rallies. My massive desk dominated the space. Kendyl closed the door, the latch clicking into place. The dim light from the desk lamp cast shadows across her alluring face. She perched on the edge of the desk, her red dress slightly riding up her soft brown thighs. Her eyes sparkled, a mix of tipsiness and anticipation.

"Tonight was incredible," she said, her voice a velvet whisper. "I forgot how much fun we used to have together."

I leaned against the door, watching her. "Yeah," I agreed. "It's been too long."

She giggled, swaying a little to the muffled bass downstairs. "I might be a tad bit tipsy," she confessed. "But it's worth it. I haven't let loose like this in... *forever.*"

I gestured toward the small bar tucked in the corner. "You want some ginger ale or something? It might help."

She shook her head, her fingers tracing the edge of the desk. "No need," she murmured. "I've got my own remedy."

I inched closer, curious as to what she meant. "And what's that?"

Before I could react, she pulled me closer, her lips meeting mine in a messy, wet connection. The kiss was a blend of lust and desire, a promise of what lay ahead if we didn't find some composure. My hands found their way to her small waist, pulling her to the edge of the desk. She encircled her smooth legs around me.

When our lips finally broke apart, she grinned. "You, Cyrus Bailey, are the only cure I need." she panted as her eyes danced with desire.

On the way home, I stopped to get gas. The gas station's fluorescent lights flickered overhead, casting an eerie glow on the cracked pavement. The potent smell of gasoline filled the air. I stepped up to the pump, frustration etching my features as I glanced at the out-of-order credit card machine with a note that said, *"Please see cashier to pay."*

I turned to Kendyl, sitting in the passenger seat, her eyes still a little glassy, and her body relaxed after our quickie inside my office. "You need anything from inside?" I asked, already knowing the answer.

She nodded, her voice soft. "Just a bottle of water, please. I need to sober up a bit more before we get home."

"Okay. I'll be right back."

As I walked across the cracked pavement toward the convenience store, I noticed a group of bikers—leather jackets, tattoos, and an air of unfamiliar camaraderie—leaning against their motorcycles. Their laughter carried across the lot, mixing with the distant hum of traffic. Inside the store, the air smelled of fried food, coffee, and disinfectant. The linoleum floor was scuffed and worn. A few flickering signs advertised discounted snacks and energy drinks on the mishmashed shelves filled with non-perishable foods, motor oil, and personal products. The cashier, a tired-looking middle-aged woman, sat behind a scratched-up Plexiglas partition. I grabbed a cold water bottle and approached the counter, placing it next to a stack of gossip magazines.

I exchanged a few words with her before asking for what I needed. "Let me get forty on pump six."

The register beeped, and I pocketed the receipt. As I turned to leave, I caught sight of the bikers again. They were clustered near my car. Kendyl was standing by the pump, her expression tense. One of the bikers—a burly guy with a beard—seemed to be arguing with her. Without hesitation, I raced out of the store, my heart pounding. Panic surged through my veins, drowning out reason as I stepped in front of her, facing the biker. I squared my shoulders, ready to defend Kendyl by any means necessary.

"Is there a mothafuckin problem?" I growled. "If you've got an issue, take that shit up with me—*not* her."

The biker's eyes narrowed, assessing me. That was when I noticed the patches on his leather jacket. It bore the unmistakable emblem of the Raging Vipers—a snarling viper with bloodied fangs. Our eyes locked, and the tension crackled like fireworks. I knew our encounter was no coincidence; it was a reckoning, a declaration of war for the death of their president.

The Raging Vipers member stepped forward, his face a mask of fury. His club members circled us like vultures, trying to perpetrate weakness. He smirked over my shoulder at Kendyl, revealing a missing bottom tooth. "You thought you could leave the club behind and not pay for what you did?" he spat, fingers brushing the handle of a concealed weapon. "You deserve worse than death, bitch."

Kendyl's eyes gleamed with rage. "And what do you deserve for kidnapping me and my child, huh?"

My stern voice cut through the tension. "Kendyl, get back in the car!" She hesitated, torn between fear and defiance, as she stood wide-eyed. But the steel in my glare left no room for negotiation. She stumbled backward, her heart pounding as fear and relief danced across her face.

My jaw tightened. Since taking over the role as president, I hadn't had to put my hands on a nigga in a minute. I missed it. "Give me a reason to beat your mothafuckin ass. I want you to," I warned.

"That bitch killed one of our own! This is mothafuckin war!"

"Call her a bitch one more time, and I'll—"

Then, the unthinkable happened—the jarring sound of gunshots rang out. The air thickened with dread. In that split second, the world narrowed to a single point: Kendyl pressing her trembling hands against the window, helpless as my body hit the pavement with a sickening thud. The bikers scattered like startled seagulls, their boots pounding against the asphalt. The shots were a cruel twist of fate—an eruption of violence during the most incredible night of my life.

A scream tore from her throat as my blood stained the pavement. I felt an instant stinging and numbing sensation as if my entire body had been set on fire. I clutched my chest and lifted my trembling hand to see crimson seeping through my fingers. The sound of her screams became louder as she sprinted toward me, unmindful of any lingering danger. She crouched down, her hands trembling as she cradled my head. Blood seeped through my shirt, staining her fingers.

"Stay with me, Cy," she pleaded, her voice raw. "Please, stay with me! I can't lose you. I can't lose you again!"

Panic clawed at my chest. The last thing I wanted to do was leave her. She fumbled for her phone, dialing for help with shaking fingers. The operator's voice sounded distant as if she were in outer space, or maybe it was the feeling of my soul leaving my body. My chest heaved with ragged breaths, each one a struggle against the encroaching darkness. The pain radiated from the gunshot wounds that pierced my body.

I looked up at her as she cradled my head with tears streaming down her cheeks. For a moment, I wondered if I'd glimpsed eternity. She was scared. I could see it all over her face. Yet, I'd never seen her look so beautiful. Her features were ethereal—soft, yet sharp, like the edges of a dream. Her eyes held clusters of wonder within, and the strands of her dark curls seemed spun from stardust. A white glow enveloped her, casting a halo around her silhouette. It was as if she'd stepped out of heaven, sent to guide me through my final passage. Her tears fell, each droplet catching the dim light and refracting it into a thousand tiny rainbows. They looked like diamonds—priceless and rare.

As I gazed up at her, my pain receded, replaced by peace. The chaos faded, leaving only her presence—the warmth of her touch, the whispered promises of forever. In that splintered moment, I believed she was my salvation, the bridge between life and whatever lay beyond for me.

My lips moved slowly, and Kendyl leaned in, desperate to catch my words. My voice faltered, and she stared at my lips, desperate to catch every syllable.

"I–I," I murmured, my grip weakening.

Kendyl shook her head, tears blurring her vision. "Don't talk, baby. Save your strength."

But I pressed on, urgency weighing on me. "I love you," I whispered, blood bubbling at my lips. "Always."

Then the world blurred, and the darkness closed in, fading everything to black.

Kendyl

Sirens wailed in the distance, but time moved too slowly—a harsh balance between life and death. I could still hear the echo of gunshots and smell the gunpowder haunting the air. The whirring grew louder as the lights flashed blue and red against the gas station's grimy windows. Soon, the paramedics swarmed around us. I clung to Cy's body, my heart a fractured strain of grief and rage.

Cy and I had shared an evening that would be forever etched in my mind. If life had shown me anything, our time on earth was too short, and vengeance *always* had its price. I couldn't say I never thought the Raging Vipers wouldn't come after me for killing Demon, but I never thought they'd come back like that.

The ambulance darted through the streets, its siren wailing like a distressed plea in the night. Inside, I clung to Cy's still hand, my knuckles white with fear. His face was expressionless, lips tinged red with blood, as the paramedics worked frantically to stabilize him.

"H-how's he doing? Is he going to survive? Please tell me he's going to survive!" I pleaded.

"He's flatlined twice," one of the paramedics muttered, sweat beading on his forehead. "We're doing everything we can."

My heart pounded in rhythm with the ambulance's jolting movements. I whispered prayers, my breath hitching as we pulled into the hospital's emergency bay. The doors swung open, and a team of doctors and nurses swarmed around us, whisking Cy away on a stretcher.

"Ma'am, you'll have to wait here," a nurse said gently, guiding me toward the waiting room before handing me the bag of Cy's belongings. "We'll update you as soon as we can."

I sank into a plastic chair, my mind a whirlwind of anxiety and hope as Cy fought for his survival. I pulled out my phone, trembling fingers dialing his sister's number.

"Nina," I said when the call connected, my voice raw. "It's Kendyl. There's been an accident. Cy got shot—twice. We're at the hospital. They're operating on him now."

Nina's gasp echoed through the phone. "*What?* Oh my God. Is he going to be okay?"

"I don't know," I admitted, tears blurring my vision. "He flatlined twice in the ambulance. But all they keep saying is they're doing everything they can."

"Oh my God! Oh my God! Okay," Nina's voice cracked. "Which hospital are you at?"

"Lakeside Memorial," I answered. "Is Cree asleep?"

"Yeah. He's been out for about forty-five minutes now."

"I want you to be here, but I don't want Cree around all this. He's already been around too much death."

"Okay. I'll stay here with him. Did you call The Spades?"

I sighed. "No."

"Make the call, Kendyl. They need to know, too."

"Okay."

"Call me back."

"I'll keep you updated, I promise."

I hung up, and the waiting room seemed to close in on me. I

pulled Cy's phone out of the plastic bag the nurse had given me. As soon as I flipped it over, the screen lit up with a call from Nitro.

My chest deflated with a hard sigh before I answered. "H-hello?" I answered wearily.

"Who is this?"

"This is Kendyl. Cy–Chop is... he's in surgery."

"He what?" he roared into the receiver.

I pulled the phone away from my ear for a second. "It was the Raging Vipers. They shot him at a gas station when we left the club-house. This is all my fault!" I sobbed.

"Which hospital are you at?"

"Lakeside Memorial."

"We're on the way," he replied before ending the call.

I clasped my hands together, praying for strength—for Cy, our son, and the fragile thread that held us together. Minutes stretched into hours. Finally, a weary doctor emerged, his eyes kind but burdened.

"He's still in surgery," he said. "The bullets caused significant damage, but we're doing our best."

I nodded, my throat too tight for words. I sank back into the chair, staring at the sterile walls. In that waiting room, time lost all meaning. Thoughts of Cree—our precious little boy who loved superheroes and bedtime stories raced through my mind. I thought of Cy's smile, his laughter, the way he'd hold me close at night. *I can't lose him. I can't. I won't.*

HOURS LATER, THE SUN HAD RISEN, AND THE HOSPITAL corridors buzzed with tension as leather-clad men lined the halls, their tattoos and grim expressions starkly contrasting the sterile surroundings. The Spades MC club members—brothers in arms— had rallied overnight with me, their loyalty unwavering. They brought food and picked up his car from the gas station. They knew the man lying in the operating room wasn't just their president; he was family.

I walked out to meet Nina in the parking lot. Cree clung to her hand, eyes wide with confusion. Nina's face mirrored my worry, lines etched by the sleepless night and shared grief.

"Thank you for being here," I whispered, my voice fragile as we hugged. "For bringing Cree."

Nina nodded, her gaze lingering on him. "I know you didn't want him here, but he woke up asking for you."

I sighed. "He's been through so much already."

She reached out and grabbed my hand. "We'll get through this, too."

Inside, the waiting room overflowed with tension. I reclaimed my seat on a plastic chair, with Cree nestled against my chest. I stroked his hair, trying to shield him from the fear that hung heavy over us all. Things had finally felt normal—our little family finding its rhythm—before my past caught up to us.

Cree shifted, his eyes welling up as he looked around. "Mommy," he whispered, "I don't want Daddy to die. I just got him."

His tiny plea shattered my heart. I pulled him closer and rocked him, tears blurring my vision. "We won't let that happen," I promised, my voice hoarse. "Your daddy's strong. He'll fight."

Nina appeared with a small bag of crackers in hand. "Hey, buddy," she said, crouching down. "Want a snack?"

Cree sniffled before accepting the crackers. His eyes darted between us, seeking reassurance. Nina took his hand, her distraction giving me a moment to collect myself. And then Nitro approached—a mountain of a man with a grizzled beard and eyes that held both menace and compassion. He sat beside me, his black leather jacket creaking with every gesture.

"You doin' alright?"

I slowly swung my head in a no. "I feel numb."

"We're family," he said, his voice gravelly. "We'll take care of you both. Whatever you need."

I nodded, gratitude swelling in my chest. "He's a fighter," I whispered, reassuring myself. "He'll pull through. He *has* to."

His grip on my shoulder was firm. "Damn right," he said. "And when he does, we'll be right here, ready to welcome him home."

At that moment, surrounded by leather jackets and an outpour of unwavering support, I felt something shift. I didn't feel alone anymore. I was a part of Cy's brotherhood—a fierce, loyal bond that transcended bloodlines and bullets. The Spades had become my makeshift family, bringing smiles to my face as they shared stories about Cy with laughter and silent nods.

"Thank you," I murmured, my voice choking. "For everything."

He nodded, eyes scanning the hallway where the white-coated doctors moved like ghosts. "We've got your back," he confirmed.

I counted the seconds between each time I rushed to the nurses' station for an update. I walked the hospital corridors, tracing invisible paths, seeking solace in the rhythm of my footsteps—anything to help pass the time. I even slipped into the chapel—finding solace in the quiet sanctuary as I sat on the small pews and prayed to the universe: *Let him live. Let him come back to us.* I didn't know if anyone was listening on the other side, but I spilled my heart there—the raw, unfiltered ache. I breathed—deep, deliberate inhales—as if oxygen had the power to ward off the fear crippling my body.

On my walk back to the waiting room, the surgeon emerged, his mask dangling from one ear. Nina and I raced toward him, our eyes wide with anticipation as The Spades stood at our backs. My hands trembled, and Nina's fingers clenched the edge of her jacket. We'd been waiting for *hours*, praying that Cy would survive the gunshot wounds and pull through surgery.

"Are you two the family of Cyrus Bailey?" the surgeon asked, his voice steady but weary.

"Yes!" I blurted out.

"Please tell me my brother is going to be okay," Nina pleaded.

"Your brother lost a significant amount of blood and required urgent surgical intervention. The bullets pierced his chest and grazed his heart. It was touch-and-go in the operating room, but we managed to stop the bleeding and remove the bullets."

My breath caught. I had imagined the worst—losing Cy, the man I'd never stopped loving—but there was a rainbow at the end of our storm. "Is he going to be okay?" I probed, my voice barely audible.

The surgeon nodded. "He's stable now. We've stitched up the wounds, and he's in recovery. But he'll need time to heal—possibly a few weeks of therapy and frequent check-ins with the cardiologist. It won't be an easy recovery, but he's strong."

Nina's eyes filled with tears. "Thank God," she whispered. "We were so scared. Can we see him?"

The surgeon glanced at the hallway behind him. "He's not awake yet, and once he does, he'll be groggy from the medicine. He's being moved to the fifth floor—room fifty-one-seventy-three."

Nina turned to me. "You go, Kendyl. I know you're the first face he's gonna want to see when he wakes up."

I took the elevator up to the fifth floor. My heart raced as my heels click-clacked down the corridor in search of his room. I pushed open the door. Cy's hospital room was faintly lit. The painted walls were a pale shade of blue, and the smell of hospital food wafted in from the hallway, mixing with the faint scent of disinfectant. A narrow window allowed a sliver of daylight to filter, casting a soft glow on the white linoleum floor. Monitors and IV lines surrounded the bed where Cy lay eerily still. He lay there, wounded and vulnerable but alive. Seeing him filled me with a whirlwind of emotions— fear of loss, gratitude for his survival, and the overwhelming desire to be by his side.

The rhythmic beeping of machines punctuated the silence, amplifying my anxiety. A chair sat by the bedside, its vinyl upholstery cracked from years of use. The patterned curtains were drawn, shielding Cy from the outside world as he fought to recover. I stood there, my heart wedged in my throat, taking in every detail—the cold lighting, the outdated family magazines on the side table, and the framed landscape painting that seemed out of place in the stark room.

I wanted to touch him, reassure myself that he was real, that he'd made it through. Above all else, I wanted to tell him how much I loved him, how I'd never stopped—anything to bridge the gap of uncertainty that had kept us apart for far too long.

My fingers intertwined with his, and I felt the warmth of his skin against mine. His hand was rough, calloused from years of hard work and the rugged life he led. Yet, beneath the roughness, there was a tenderness—a vulnerability that made my heart ache to hear his voice or feel him squeeze my hand. I traced the lines on his palm, feeling the pulse beneath my touch. It was an unbreakable connection. And in that moment, I vowed to stop running and hold on tight, no matter what lay ahead.

My tear-streaked face hovered above him. "Don't you ever scare me like that again. I thought I'd lost you," I choked out, my heart overflowing. "I love you, Cy. I never stopped loving you. I don't want to spend another minute not talking about it or figuring out what to say and what not to say. So, if you pull through, my answer is yes. You hear me, Cy? My answer is yes! I will marry you."

A few seconds passed before his eyes slowly fluttered open. They were red-rimmed and glassy. My fingers trembled as I held his hand.

"Oh my God, Cy. Hey," I whispered.

His voice was raspy and dry. "Did they get 'em?" he queried, his anger simmering below the surface. "The mothafucka who shot me?"

"Shh. It's okay, baby. You're safe now."

He clenched his jaw. I could see the urge to retaliate burning in his veins. "Kendyl, tell me."

I sighed, my expression pained. "The club's handling it. But you need to stay calm. You're not strong enough for war right now."

The room fell silent for a second. "I dreamed you said you'd marry me," he blurted out.

My lips curved into a soft smile. "That wasn't a dream," I replied. "I told you yes just before you opened your eyes."

"It wasn't a dream?"

"No, baby," I murmured. "It wasn't."

I watched his anger melt away, replaced by wonder as a weak smile tugged at his lips. "You're gonna marry a nigga?"

I leaned in, brushing my lips against his forehead. "As long as you promise to leave the retaliation to The Spades," I bargained. "I need you all in one piece if you're gonna meet me down that aisle one day."

"I love you," he whispered before pointing to the locket around his neck. "Take it off. It's yours again. I'll get you a real ring when I'm out of here."

Kendyl

T*wo and a half weeks later.*

It was mid-afternoon when I pulled up to the hospital entrance. My heart galloped against my ribs. It had been two and a half weeks of waiting, decorating our home, and planning Cy's perfect welcome home party. He'd been through hell, but he was finally coming back to me. During those weeks in the hospital, Cy's mindset was a rollercoaster of emotions. At first, his pain, frustration, and thirst for revenge consumed him—the physical agony of his healing wounds, the helplessness of being confined to a hospital bed and wearing a heart monitor. But as the days stretched on, he found solace in the fact that he was getting better and stronger daily, inching him closer to the moment he'd be reunited with the roar of his motorcycle and the wind tearing through his locs.

Cy emerged from the hospital doors with an orderly by his side holding a bouquet of get-well-soon balloons. His smile when he saw me waiting by the passenger side door was worth every sleepless night. I rushed to his side, wrapping my arms around him.

"Welcome home," I whispered, my voice thick with emotion.

"Thank you."

My hands trembled with excitement as I helped him into the car. We drove in silence, Cy's hand resting on mine. When we pulled up to The Spades clubhouse, he raised an eyebrow.

"What's going on, Kendyl?"

I grinned. "Just trust me."

We walked inside, and the room erupted. "*Surprise!*" The chorus of voices enveloped us. Cy's brown eyes widened as he took in the scene: banners, twinkling lights, and smiling familiar faces. His eyes filled with tears as the room buzzed with laughter and chatter, the scent of leather filling the air. His MC brothers clapped him on the back one by one, and Nina wiped away happy tears as she held up our son. Cree held his tiny arms in the air, clutching a poster he'd decorated that read, "Welcome Home, Daddy."

Nina put him down, and he shuffled toward Cy. His tiny face lit up with joy, and Cy scooped him into his arms. "Hey, champ," he whispered. "I missed you."

I noticed his parents standing near the cake table. Tears raced down their faces as they watched their son—their biker son—surrounded by this unconventional family. He grabbed my hand and walked us over to introduce them to our son, their grandson, for the first time.

His mother hugged him tightly. "We're so thankful you're back on your feet, son. We've been praying for your recovery."

His father nodded. "You're a fighter, just like your old man."

Cy's gaze shifted to me. "Mom, Dad, y'all remember Kendyl? Well, I want you to meet our son, Cree," he proudly announced.

His mother beamed. "Well, well! Look at him. Those beautiful Bailey men eyes—just like yours and your father's, Cyrus."

"He's perfect, isn't he?" Nina asked, joining the five of us.

"That he is," his mother agreed, gently pinching Cree's plump cheek. "Hi there, little one. I'm your grandma Margaret."

"And I'm your papa James," his father added with a warm smile.

Cy cleared his throat. "There's more, Mom, Dad. Kendyl and I… we're getting married," he announced, voice echoing through the room.

The entire place erupted. Bikers whooped, beers and drinks sloshing. They'd seen our love story unfold from beginning to end, with all the good, bad, and ugly in between.

"Chop's tying the knot!" Nitro chanted.

"Welcome to the club, Chop!" Harlan added, raising his glass.

"Our boy's found his ride-or-die," someone in the crowd called out.

The DJ cued up "Let's Get Married" by Jagged Edge, and the beat pulsed through the room. Cy pulled me close, spinning me around as we danced. His MC brothers and family joined in, swaying and celebrating. My heart pounded with joy. Our love was as wild as the open road. We'd fought for our second chance, and in that moment, surrounded by the people we loved most, it couldn't have felt more meant to be.

The room blurred into a sea of tattoos, laughter, and the promise of forever. Chop pulled me aside mid-song, away from the crowd, his fingers brushing against mine. "I can't thank you enough," he said, his voice rough with emotion. "For everything. You held me down when I was at my lowest. I love you."

My lips spread into a warm smile, my heart swelling as tears welled up. "I love you so much," I whispered.

"C'mon, let's go outside and get some fresh air," he suggested.

As we left the clubhouse, Cy wrapped his arms around me. The wind whipped through our hair as he leaned in close, pinning my back against the driver's side door.

"You know what? This party was amazing, but there's something else I've been waiting to do."

I raised an eyebrow. "What's that?"

He grinned. "Show you just how much I missed you."

With that, we sped off into the night, leaving the cheers and laughter behind. My heart was whole, knowing our love had withstood the storm and emerged stronger on the other side.

Four weeks later.

I PUSHED MY CART DOWN THE FEMININE CARE AISLE IN THE grocery store. The shelves were lined with pastel-colored boxes, each promising answers to my life-altering question: *Am I pregnant?* I quickly glanced around, hoping no one was paying attention. My heart raced as I picked up the pregnancy test, tucking it discreetly into my basket. I didn't want to make a big deal out of it until I knew for sure.

After purchasing the test, I headed to the back of the store for the bathroom. The public restroom door creaked as I entered, catching my reflection in the mirror. The harsh fluorescent light revealed every line and dark circle on my face. I drew in a deep breath before disappearing behind the stall. Three minutes of waiting felt like an eternity. I leaned against the cold tile, my mind racing. Memories flooded back—the last time I'd stood in that position, staring at a similar plastic stick, my entire world shifted on its axis. Back then, I was alone, scared, and anxious. But this time was different. This time, I felt a flutter of hope in the pit of my stomach. A tiny spark ignited inside my chest.

When I finally dared to look, the two pink lines stared back at me, confirming what my heart already knew. I was pregnant *again*. I left the restroom, my steps lighter, and left the store to pick up Cree from daycare. It had been the two of us for so long that I wondered if my heart was big enough to love another child. But the minute those two lines appeared, it was as if my heart doubled in size. I couldn't wait to see Cree's chubby cheeks flush with excitement when he learned he would be a big brother.

———

I ARRIVED AT HIS DAYCARE AND FOUND HIM IN THE MIDDLE OF an activity, putting together a puzzle with another kid in his class. I stood at the doorway, silently watching him interact with other kids his age.

"Cree, your mommy's here," his teacher announced.

His face lit up when he saw me before he waved goodbye to his friends and teachers. We inched over to his cubby to grab his back-pack and jacket.

"Guess what, Cree?" I beamed as we walked hand-in-hand back to the car.

"What?"

I knelt to his level, brushing his curls from his face. "Mommy's going to have another baby," I explained.

His little face lit up. "You're having a baby?" he asked, his voice high-pitched.

"Yes. You're going to be a big brother!" I squealed.

He patted my flat stomach as if saying hello to his new little brother or sister. "Hi, baby."

Cree's reaction to the news was a pleasant mix of curiosity and excitement, which brought a smile to my face. "I think we should see daddy and tell him the good news. What do you think?"

"Yeah!"

"Okay, baby boy. Let's go."

My heart swelled with joy as I drove toward the clubhouse, eager to tell Cy the news about our growing family. I knew navigating life with a toddler and a new baby would be the most incredible adven-ture we'd ever embark upon—a legacy beyond leather and steel.

Chop

Whoever said bullets don't discriminate was right. They didn't give a fuck about your past, your goals, or your deepest regrets. All they did was mercilessly tear through flesh and bone. That first shot was sharp and sudden. The second almost sent me to heaven's doorstep. The doctors did their magic, stitching me back together. They cited words like "phenomenon" and "luck." But I couldn't give a fuck less about their words. I knew the scars would fade, but the vengeance that gnawed at my soul only got stronger as the days passed. My only refuge from the darkness was *her*. Kendyl—my rock. She'd sat by my bedside and helped nurse me back to health while still holding down the house and raising our son.

I'd stared death in the face and emerged whole through the flames. I'd seen my life flash before my eyes—the fights, the bloodshed. Maybe this was my second chance. To love harder. To fight back. To spend the rest of my life with the woman I'd never stopped loving. But now that I was out, I wondered what would come next. Would my family ever feel safe again knowing the man who shot me was still out there? Could I ride down the street without feeling like I was going to jump out of my skin at every turn? Rage consumed me, and I'd reveled in it since waking up after my surgery.

I'd been dealing with club business all day—the typical mayhem that came with being the head of The Spades. I called a small meeting to gather my inner circle of brothers in the clubhouse. I stood behind my desk, studying the map spread out before me. The Raging Vipers MC club shooter had been laying low since the night he shot me, and shit had been too quiet. He'd put two bullets in my chest, and the debt remained unpaid.

My gaze swept over their faces—the enforcer, the road captain, the medic. They waited patiently, expecting orders from me. "What's the latest update, Nitro?" I asked, my voice slicing through the silence.

Nitro stood across from me, a scar tracing his jawline. "We've still got eyes on their clubhouse and got riders set up near all the city entrances," he said, jabbing at different locations on the map. "But the VP, Blade—the one who shot you—he's like a mothafuckin ghost."

I grunted. "Keep watching," I ordered. "And when you find him, bring his ass straight to me. I want him alive and squirming."

As my men shuffled out of my office, the door creaked open. I glanced up, expecting to see another club member. Instead, it was Kendyl holding Cree's hand. She wore a tight black tank top, her wild, curly hair cascading over her shoulders. Cree's eyes widened at my patched leather jacket clinging to my shoulders.

"Hey," she said softly. "Did I catch you at a bad time?"

I shook my head while pushing my thoughts of revenge aside. "Never when it's you two."

"Daddy!" Cree squealed, racing around the desk to hug me. He darted over, his chubby fingers reaching for my beard. I scooped him up, the weight of fatherhood rooting me. Kendyl walked around and perched on the edge of my desk, concern etching her melanated features.

"You're tense," she said. "What's going on?"

I hesitated. I'd wanted to keep the club life separate from my family, but she deserved to know the truth. "The Raging Vipers," I admitted. "They're up to something. I can feel that shit in my gut," I explained, my gravelly voice echoing off the walls.

She leaned in and traced the scar on my chest through my clothes. "Baby, you survived for a reason. Maybe it's time to find a different path."

I watched Cree play with his toy motorcycle by the door. His joyous laughter filled the room, a stark contrast to the violence brewing within me. I looked at the map, the red pins marking the Raging Vipers' hideouts. "I tried, but I can't let it go. It's got a crazy hold on me."

"Well, maybe my news will change your mind."

My shoulders tensed as I leaned back in my chair, intrigued but cautious. "What's wrong?"

She smiled while resting her hand on her stomach. "Nothing's wrong. Actually, everything's right for the first time in a long time."

"What do you mean?"

Kendyl hesitated, her mocha brown eyes locking onto mine as she breathed deeply. "Cy, I'm pregnant."

I stood, knocking my chair back. My heart stuttered. Another child—a brother or sister for Cree. I'd faced bullets, power struggles, and betrayal, but Kendyl's news shook me to my core. The thought of tiny shoes, bedtime stories, and teaching a new life to ride a bike all fluttered to the front of my mind. I'd finally have a chance to be there for everything I missed with my firstborn. I couldn't wait to witness Kendyl's belly swell with the new life growing inside her.

"Pregnant? Kendyl, you're—"

"Yes. We're going to have another baby, Cy. Are you happy?"

I pulled her delicate body into my arms, stroking her cheek before kissing her with a force that was both fierce and tender. "Happy?" I asked when I pulled away. "I'm excited as hell for our new lil rider."

The Spades would always be my blood, but now I had a different legacy to protect. With that thought in mind, I walked around my desk and opened the drawer, revealing a red velvet ring box. I traced its soft edges, my heartbeat racing.

Kendyl's eyes widened when she noticed the box in my hand. "What's that?"

I inched around the desk and sank to one knee in front of her, the old floorboards creaking underneath my weight. I cracked open the box, revealing a vintage engagement ring that had once been my grandmother's. My mother had slid it to me at my welcome home party, and I'd been secretly working to have it resized and fitted with new diamonds.

"Kendyl," I said, my voice gruff. "I think I owe you this."

Kendyl gasped, tears welling in her eyes. "Cy, you don't—"

I cut her off. "No, listen," I said as I slid the ring onto her finger. "I've loved you since the moment you walked into my life. You're fierce, strong, and beautiful, and you've got a heart as wild and pure as gold." She blinked, speechless, allowing me the space to continue. "I want you to be my wife," I confirmed. "Not just because of the new baby, but because I can't imagine going another day of my life without you having my last name."

Her nervous laughter bubbled up, joy spilling over. "Yes! Oh my God, baby! Yes!"

***

LATER THAT NIGHT, MY VIBRATING PHONE PIERCED THE SILENCE of my bedroom. I reached for it, my pulse quickening as I put it to my ear. Nitro's familiar voice crackled through the line, delivering news that sent adrenaline surging through me.

"We found him, Chop. The bitch ass nigga who shot you. He's at the warehouse."

My grip tightened. The mothafucka who'd nearly taken me away from my family—the one who'd left me bleeding out on the gas station pavement, gasping for air—was finally within reach. The taste of revenge was more bitter than sweet, but it was a dish I'd been waiting to serve since I woke up in that fuckin' hospital bed.

I flipped the sheets off and slipped out of bed, careful not to wake Kendyl. Her soft breaths, the warmth of her naked brown body—it all anchored me. But duty called, and I couldn't ignore that shit. I dressed in black, the leather and bulletproof vest clinging to my tattooed skin like a coat of armor.

I leaned over Kendyl, brushing a gentle kiss against her forehead. "I'm coming back to you. I promise," I whispered.

She stirred, eyes fluttering open. "Cy," she whispered, her voice thick with sleep. "W-where are you going?"

"They got him, and I need to finish this," I said sternly before I pulled her close, and our lips met in a sweet kiss. "I love you."

Her chest deflated in a sharp sigh. The disapproving look in her eyes told me she wasn't happy with my decision but knew there was nothing she could do to stop me. Her delicate fingers traced the location of the scar on my chest—the one that still ached from time to time.

"Just... promise me you'll be safe," she said, eyes searching mine. "Do what you have to do to make it back to me—to *us*."

I nodded, my heart heavy as I cupped her cheek. "Always. I'll fight my way through hell if I have to."

Outside, the engine roared as I straddled my bike. I looked back at the house. Kendyl and Cree slept inside, peaceful and unharmed. I could've killed the engine, trekked back inside, and crawled into bed. I could've made the call to let Nitro and my men handle it all. But I couldn't let it go. I'd made a choice—to face the past, to claim my vengeance.

After a brief drive, the warehouse came into view. My boots echoed on the concrete floor as I stepped inside, my gun in hand and my chest protected with a bulletproof vest. My men stood guard, their faces grim and their loyalty unwavering, ready for war. The shooter—a rat-faced fuck boy named Blade—was bound and bloodied, rage in his eyes. I circled him, memories of that night seeping into the forefront of my mind. I saw the despair across Kendyl's face. I felt the coldness of the pavement against my skin. I tasted the blood pooling at my lips.

I lunged forward, the gun in my hand gleaming. "This is the second time you tried to take something from me—first my girl and my son, then my fuckin' life," I growled.

Blade spat, defiance in his beady ass eyes. "Fuck you and The Spades! Raging Vipers 'til I die, bitch! You won't break me!"

I didn't want to break him. I wanted closure. I wanted satisfaction. I wanted to deliver the slowest, most agonizing death possible. It was the least he deserved. Instead of paying him back in bullets like he'd done me, I put my gun back in the holster and pulled out a blade. Under the flickering light, I carved The Spades emblem into his bleeding flesh—the pain an ugly mirror of my own, before stabbing him in the chest repeatedly until he bled out.

When I was sure he'd taken his final breath, I had my men tie a rope to his legs and hook him to the back of my bike. My motorcycle roared to life, the night air biting at my skin. I rode, the wind whipping through my locs as I dragged his body through the gravel, allowing the jagged rocks to peel away his flesh as the weightless feeling of relief washed over me.

Once all the rage left my body, I stopped and allowed my men to discard his remains. As I approached the house, the motion-sensor porch light flickered on. I dismounted my bike and shed my leather jacket before crossing the threshold into the quiet house. I stripped at the door, tossing my bloodied clothes in a garbage bag and taking a long, hot shower before crawling back into bed beside Kendyl.

"You're home," she whispered, pulling me into a desperate kiss.

"Told you I would be. I'll always come back to you," I murmured against her lips.

Epilogue

Kendyl

Seven months later.

After finding out my pregnancy was high-risk, I spent most of my second and third trimesters on bed rest. As much as I pushed to delay the wedding until after I delivered, Cy insisted we tie the knot before the baby arrived. He wanted us to be a real family on paper, all four of us. I finally agreed because I longed for a sense of normalcy and had gotten the green light from my doctors. I would become Mrs. Cyrus Bailey, come hell or high water.

I looked in the mirror, applying a final coat of my nude lipstick before replacing the cap. The loose spiral curls framing my face and pearls adorning my ears added an air of sophistication to my overall look. My bronzed cheeks glowed with happiness. My eyes sparkled with anticipation as I smoothed my hand over my round belly.

I gave myself one last onceover before grabbing my bouquet and waddling to the door. "It's showtime, baby girl."

The music played as I emerged from the back into the sea of

leather lining the silver Chiavari chairs around me. With the help of their parents and The Spades, Cy and his sister Nina helped to transform the clubhouse into a makeshift chapel with twinkling fairy lights adorning the rafters and flickering candles at each row of chairs. Cy stood at the altar, his patched leather jacket replaced with a tailored suit. His freshly twisted locs were pulled back, and his crisp shirt was slightly unbuttoned, revealing the tip of the scar across his chest—the mark of survival. My heart raced, not from fear, but from eagerness.

I walked down the aisle with my long curls cascading over my ivory maternity gown. My eyes locked onto Cy's, and the whole world narrowed to just the two of us. He'd seen me at my lowest, darkest moments, and we'd managed to find love again through the bullet wounds and blood. We were made for each other. I reached out to grab his hand as The Spades—inked and loyal—watched us, their respect evident as the preacher began.

He cleared his throat. "Dearly beloved, we are gathered here today to witness the union of Cyrus 'Chop' Bailey and Kendyl Parker."

When it was time to say our vows, Cy raised my hand to his lips and gently kissed it, the softness of his lips brushing against my trembling limb. "Kendyl," he said, his voice steady and sure. "You're my compass. You've been my rock and my salvation. From this day forward, I promise to cherish and protect you until my dying breath."

My eyes shimmered with unshed tears. "Cy," I whispered. "You're my anchor. You've shown me love in the middle of my chaos and a level of tenderness my heart has never known. I promise to stand by your side and ride shotgun throughout this life with you, no matter what comes our way."

We exchanged rings, and before I knew it, the preacher declared us husband and wife. Cy kissed me with so much passion it made my toes curl. As we inched down the aisle, fingers laced together, the clubhouse erupted in cheers and whistles.

At our reception, guests danced, drank, and clinked their glasses, toasting our second chance at love—a rareness in the biker world. As the night wore on, I felt a sudden, sharp pain in my abdomen. Initially, I brushed it off as nerves, attributing it to the excitement and chaos of the evening. But the pain intensified, causing me to grip the edge of our newlywed table for support. On cue, Cy rushed to my side with concern etched across his handsome face.

"Baby, are you okay?" he asked, guiding me toward the chair.

"I... I think I'm in labor," I gasped, my eyes wide.

Cy's jaw dropped. "*Labor?* Oh shit. We're in the middle of our reception!"

I nodded as I braced for my next contraction. "I know, but our little girl is eager to meet us. She can't wait any longer."

Without saying another word, we hurriedly made our way to the car, my short train trailing behind me. Our guests watched in surprise, rallying around us, sending well wishes, and eagerly awaiting birthing updates as we hurried to the emergency room, still in our wedding attire. The unexpected twist of going into labor at our reception added a memorable chapter to our wedding, making it a day I was sure we'd never forget.

***

Chop

I followed closely behind Kendyl at the hospital as the nurse wheeled her up to the labor and delivery wing. The medical team worked swiftly to get her hooked up and monitored by the machines. And after four pushes, our daughter arrived—a tiny bundle of sweet brown joy weighing five and a half pounds. Although she'd made her debut six weeks earlier than anticipated, she was perfectly healthy. Kendyl cradled her close, tears streaming down her face. I stood by her side, equally emotional and grateful. But the real magic happened when Nina brought Cree to meet the baby in the recovery room. My heart swelled as I watched him peek through the door. His eyes widened at the sight of the baby in Kendyl's arms.

"Mommy, who's that?" Cree queried, his voice a mix of curiosity and awe.

Kendyl smiled. "Cree, this is your baby sister, Novah. Today's her birthday."

Cree inched closer, his little fingers touching the baby's cheek. "Novah?" he whispered as if testing the word.

"Yes," Kendyl said, her voice tender. "You're a big brother now! Are you excited?"

Cree's eyes sparkled. "She's tiny."

Kendyl nodded. "And she's going to need lots of love from her big brother as she grows up and gets bigger."

Cree leaned in and planted a gentle kiss on the baby's forehead. "Hi, baby Novah," he said, his tiny voice sounding sweet as pie. Kendyl and I exchanged a knowing glance, hearts silently overflowing with gratitude. Our wedding reception may have taken an unexpected turn, but it was a twist I'd cherish for the rest of my life. Life had given me the most beautiful wedding gift—a wife, a daughter, and a son, all bound by love and brand new beginnings.

THE END

Afterword

A note from K.L. Hall.

Reader,

Thank you for reading "Bound in the Arms of a Thug: Chop & Kendyl's Love Story." If you've made it this far, I hope you'll consider telling me what you thought about the book in the form of a **five-star review and/or rating**. Don't hesitate to let me know what you'd like to see from me next! I thoroughly enjoy reading your thoughts and hearing from you as well! I'm always striving to attract new readers and retain current ones, and reviews are one of the easiest ways to attract readers. If you loved the book, tell a friend, and most importantly, let me know!

All my love,
K.L. Hall

About the Author

K.L. Hall is a national bestselling and award-winning author. As a serial storyteller, Hall has penned over three dozen titles in various genres—including African American urban fiction and romance, paranormal, children's books (as Kimberley M.), and non-fiction. Her fictional stories straddle the intersection of classic Urban and spellbinding Romance.

Highly Acclaimed Titles:
In the Arms of a Savage: (Peaked at #1 in Women's Fiction)
The Potomac Falls Series (Peaked at #1 and #2 in African American Erotica)

Sign up for my mailing list to stay updated with new releases, giveaways, sneak peeks, and more! Click this link: https://bit.ly/38RMpV5

Connect with me on social media:
Facebook: https://www.facebook.com/authorklhall
Twitter: https://twitter.com/authorklhall
Instagram: https://www.instagram.com/officialklhall/
Website: https://www.authorklhall.com

Other novels by K.L. Hall:
Diary of a Hood Princess 1-3
Rise of a Street King: The Justice Silva Story (*Spin-Off to the Diary of a Hood Princess series*)

Broken Condoms and Promises 1-3

In the Arms of a Savage 1-3

Built for a Savage: Blaze and Camille's Love Story (*Spin-Off to the In the Arms of a Savage Series*)

A Ruthle$$ Love Story 1-3

Fallin' for the Alpha of the Streets 1-2

The Most Savage of Them All: The Wolfe Calloway Story (*Prequel to the In the Arms of a Savage Series*)

When a Gangsta Loves a Good Girl

Caught Between My Husband and a Hustler

The Illest Taboo 1-2

To the Only Thug I'll Ever Love

A Lover's Heist: Chief and Gianna's Love Story

A Lover's Heist II: Rome and Lira's Love Story

A Lover's Heist III: Baby and Skai's Love Story

Crushed Velvet & Cashmere

Crushed Velvet & Cashmere 2

Entanglements

Never Had a Bad Boy Love Me So Good

Good Girls Always Got a Thing for the Thugs

Professor Zaddy: A Potomac Falls Novel

Bound in the Arms of a Thug: Chop & Kendyl's Love Story

Short Reads + Novellas:

Bi-Curious: An Erotic Tale

Bi-Curious 2: Tastes Like Candy

A Savage Calloway Christmas (*Christmas novella to the In the Arms of a Savage Series*)

Lovin' the Alpha of the Streets: A Valentine's Day Novella (*Valentine's Day novella to the Fallin' for the Alpha of the Streets Series*)

Awakened: A Paranormal Romance

As Long as You Stay Down

Solace in Seven

Solace II: The Final Cut

Something Bleu

Something Borrowed

Something New

The Knight Before Christmas: A Potomac Falls Short

I'll Be Home for Christmas: A Potomac Falls Short Book II

Triggered: A Potomac Falls Novella

Wasted Off You: A Friends to Lovers Novella

Because You Don't Know My Name: A Potomac Falls Novella

Will You Say My Name: A Potomac Falls Novella Book Two

Remember My Name: A Potomac Falls Novella Book Three

Every Thug Needs a Lady: A Lady and the Tramp Retelling

Ten Things I Hate About Lovin' You: An Enemies to Lovers Novella

In Exchange: An Urban Thriller

Children's Books:

Princess for Hire

Princess Twinkle Toes & the Missing Magic Sneakers

Little One, Change the World

Adjust Your Crown: A Self-Love Coloring Book for Children of Color

Non-Fiction:

Authors are a Business: The Booked & Busy Course Mini Book

BLP

Visit bit.ly/readBLP to join our mailing list for sneak peeks and release day links!

Let's connect on social media!
Facebook - B. Love Publications
Twitter - @blovepub
Instagram - @blovepublications

We hate errors, but we are human! If the B. Love team leaves any grammatical errors behind, do us a kindness and send them to us directly in an email to blovepublications@gmail.com
with ERRORS as the subject line.

As always, if you enjoyed this book, please leave a review on Amazon/Goodreads, recommend it on social media and/or to a friend, and mark it as READ on your Goodreads profile.

By the Book with B Podcast: bit.ly/bythebookwithb

148

By the Book with B Podcast: bit.ly/bythebookwithb